JESS THE BORDER COLLIE
The Discovery

Carrie was lying face down. The oily sea licked at her outstretched arm. 'Carrie!' Jenny screamed. But Carrie didn't move.

Stumbling and sliding, Jenny went towards her friend. The sea rushed in to cover the rocks, making it impossible for Jenny to see where next to step. She paused, her heart pounding so hard she could hear it. Carrie hadn't moved, in spite of the cold water splashing up against her, touching her with the oil. *Could she have struck her head when she fell? Might she drown?* Jenny thought frantically.

'Carrie!' she shrieked again. She couldn't move any faster. The waves on the rocks and the oil made it too dangerous to hurry. Then, suddenly, Jenny heard a welcome sound. She looked up.

Jess was flying across the beach towards her. His ears were up and his tail streamed out behind him in the wind. He was barking as he ran.

'Jess! Oh, Jess,' sobbed Jenny. 'Good boy! Come, come quickly...'

The DISCOVERY

LUCY DANIELS

Hodder
Children's
Books

a division of Hodder Headline

Special thanks to Ingrid Hoare

Text copyright © 2000 Working Partners Limited
Created by Working Partners Limited, London W6 0QT
Illustrations copyright © 2000 Sheila Ratcliffe
Jess the Border Collie is a trademark of Working Partners Limited

First published in Great Britain in 2000
by Hodder Children's Books

A Catalogue record for this book is available from the British Library

ISBN 0 340 77847 4

Typeset by Avon Dataset Ltd, Bidford-on-Avon, Warks

Printed and bound in Great Britain by
The Guernsey Press Co. Ltd, Channel Isles

Hodder Children's Books
a division of Hodder Headline
338 Euston Road
London NW1 3BH

1

Jenny Miles took a deep gulp of sea air. It filled her lungs and made her feel wide awake. From up here on the cliff path, she had a bird's eye view of the curving, craggy cliffs that gave Cliffbay its name, and the choppy blue water below.

The path was windswept and wild, yet bathed in soft spring sunshine. Jenny gave a little sigh of contentment. Nothing to do but enjoy these last few days of the Easter holidays with her friends, Carrie and Fiona, and Jess – her beloved Border collie.

'Wait for me!'

Jenny stopped and looked back down the path. Carrie Turner, her best friend, was lagging behind. 'Come on, sleepyhead,' Jenny called. 'Catch up with us.'

'Shall I give you a little push?' Fiona McLay teased, turning round and smiling at Carrie.

'You're walking too fast,' Carrie puffed.

'Are you OK, Carrie?' asked Jenny, as Carrie caught her up and slipped an arm through her own. Carrie had been ill recently and this was the first day she'd been out with her friends.

'I'm fine.' Carrie smiled. But she was breathing hard. 'Where's Jess?'

Jenny looked around. She spotted the white tip of the collie's plumy tail waving from a clump of undergrowth and pointed.

'He's found some enticing smell, I bet,' she laughed. 'A mouse, or something.'

'Good old Jess!' Fiona grinned.

'Is it nice to have Mrs Grace back?' Carrie asked, falling into step with Jenny and Fiona.

Ellen Grace was the housekeeper at Windy Hill, the sheep farm where Jenny lived with her father, Fraser Miles. Mrs Grace had come to look after the Mileses almost two years ago, after the death of Jenny's mother, Sheena Miles. Now, she was part of the family.

'Hmm, it's great. I had a huge, cooked breakfast this morning,' Jenny replied dreamily, patting her tummy. 'What a treat.'

'Did she have a nice time in Canada?' Fiona asked.

'She had a lovely time with her sister,' Jenny said. 'But she missed us.'

'I bet she didn't!' Carrie teased.

Jenny giggled.

'Let's start back home,' Fiona suggested. 'I'm hungry.'

'Right,' Jenny agreed. 'Jess has had enough of a walk, now.' She shouted his name and Jess's sleek white nose popped up from the grass. He put his head to one side, then, as Jenny called again, he streaked towards her, his pink tongue lolling happily. Jess could run like the wind.

'Hello, boy,' Jenny said, smiling, as the collie came up at a rush. She reached out to stroke Jess's soft head. The Border collie gazed up at her fondly. 'Come on,' said Jenny. 'Time to go home.'

It was some time before Jenny realised that Jess was not at her side. 'Jess!' Jenny exclaimed, looking around. He wasn't following, either. 'Where have you got to?' she called.

The others stopped and looked back. Jenny called again, louder this time. Fiona and Carrie shouted too. But there was no sign of him.

'It's not like Jess not to come when he's called,' Jenny said with a frown.

'Where could he be?' Fiona looked worried.

Fiona loved Jess, probably as much as Jenny did. When Fiona had become ill following a terrifying fire at Windy Hill, Jenny had let her have Jess for a while, as a companion. The fire, which had almost destroyed the farmhouse, had been Fiona's fault and the shame and guilt of what she had done had kept her off school for weeks. Jess had helped Fiona to recover, and she had been friends with Jenny ever since.

'Jess!' she yelled.

Above the sound of the wind, a faint barking could be heard. 'It's coming from down on the beach!' Jenny said. She ran towards the cliff edge and looked over.

'Can you see him?' Carrie asked, grabbing onto Jenny's T-shirt and leaning over, dangerously close to the edge. Her red hair rose round her face on the wind. But before Jenny could reply, a bark came from further down the cliff path.

'Oh . . . look!' Fiona said, sounding relieved. '*There* he is! Here he comes! He couldn't have heard us

4

calling him. Here, Jess!' She clapped her hands.

Jenny turned to look. A Border collie was trotting briskly towards them. But Jenny could tell immediately that it wasn't Jess.

'No,' she said, disappointed. 'That's not Jess. It's some other dog.' Even from a distance, she knew every inch of the collie she'd had since he was born. And this dog wasn't running the way Jess ran either.

'It's definitely a Border collie, though,' Carrie said, coming back to the path.

The dog came up. Its ears were up and its tail held straight and still. 'Hello . . .' Jenny spoke soothingly. 'Where did you come from?'

The dog's tail began to wag hesitantly. Jenny put out her hand, level with the collie's nose. She sniffed at it, then wagged her tail harder. Carrie and Fiona reached out to pet the dog too.

'She's mine,' came a voice. 'She won't hurt you.' A dark-haired boy of about their age was walking towards them. He had his hands in the pockets of his khaki shorts and the dog's lead slung round his shoulders.

'She's great. What's her name?' Carrie asked.

'Orla,' the boy answered. 'And mine's David. David Fergusson.'

'Are you on holiday?' Jenny asked him. She hadn't

seen this boy around before.

'No, we moved here just recently, to a house in Cliffbay.' David aimed a kick at a pebble and it sailed smoothly off the edge of the cliff and down to the stony shore below.

At that moment, the sound of Jess's faint barking reached them again. 'Did you hear that?' said Jenny. 'That's *my* Border collie. His name is Jess. He must have gone down the path onto the beach.'

'We've called and called,' Fiona explained. 'But he won't come back.'

'Jess usually does as he's told,' Carrie added.

'It might be that he can't find the way back up,' David suggested. 'There's only one way down. My dad and I discovered that last week.'

'It won't be that,' Jenny reasoned. 'Jess knows the beach and the cliffs really well. Something else is keeping him down there, I'm sure of it.'

Jenny went over near to the edge of the cliff and peered over again. 'Jess!' she shouted. 'Here, boy. Come on!' She yelled into the noise of the wind gusting around the rock face and wondered if Jess could hear her.

Orla stood beside her. Her ears pricked up in interest at all the shouting.

'I'll go with you down to the beach, if you like,' David said, behind her.

'Yes, it looks like we'll have to go and fetch him,' Jenny decided. She looked at Fiona, who had goosebumps all over her arms. Carrie was sitting cross-legged on the grassy verge to the path. Her chin was propped in the palm of her hand. She looked tired. Jenny felt a bit concerned, Carrie was usually so energetic and determined.

'Do you two want to go back home?' Jenny asked. 'I'll go down with . . . David,' she added, rather shyly.

Fiona looked at Carrie. 'Up to you,' she shrugged.

'No, of course we'll come.' Carrie stood up, smiling. 'Jess might need our help. Come on.'

They fell into single file, David leading the way back along the path. A fine mist had begun rolling in off the sea. Jenny's face felt moist.

'The tide's coming in,' David said over his shoulder.

Jenny felt a prickle of fear for Jess. It was so unlike him not to come when called. He had obeyed Jenny faithfully since he was a puppy. Something must be keeping him from returning to her.

Jess had been the runt of a litter produced by Nell, one of Fraser's sheepdogs. He had been born with a twisted leg and Jenny's dad had felt it kinder to put the puppy to sleep. But Jenny had pleaded with him not to. At eight weeks, an operation had put right Jess's damaged leg and since then he had led an active and happy life. Jenny adored him and had always felt protective about him.

'D'you live in Cliffbay?' David asked Jenny, interrupting her thoughts.

'No, Graston. My dad's a sheep farmer,' she told him. 'I expect you'll be going to our school – Greybridge Senior?'

'Yes,' David called back. 'What's it like?'

'It's OK,' Jenny laughed. 'We all go there. You'll survive!'

'But only if you're *lucky*,' Carrie said, then she cackled horribly, like a witch.

David laughed. 'I'm not sure if I will!' he said.

'Here's the path,' Jenny said. She stopped where a narrow opening sloped away steeply to the beach. Overgrown with gorse, its entrance was almost invisible.

'Is it safe to go down?' Fiona asked.

'We'll have to be careful,' Jenny said. 'It's probably a bit slippery.' Jenny hesitated for a moment. She looked at Carrie and then went over to her and spoke quietly. 'You're not completely better yet, are you? You don't have to come down with us, you know. You could wait up here.'

8

'I'm OK,' Carrie said brightly. She made a face at Jenny. 'Stop fussing, will you! I want to go with you. Honestly.'

'OK, if you're sure,' Jenny said. She turned back to David and Fiona, in time to see Orla begin the climb down to the beach. She was as sure-footed as a mountain goat, stepping sideways daintily, her sharp claws keeping a grip on the gravel path. David followed her.

'Jess!' called Jenny, as she went. 'Here Jess!' But Jess still didn't appear.

The winding path *was* slippery and Jenny found the best way to keep her balance was to walk with her hands outstretched, ready to grab onto the long grasses and wild flowering plants that grew among the rock.

David was ahead of her, helpfully calling out the places it was best to avoid stepping. 'Watch out – loose stone,' he warned.

Carrie had her hands round Fiona's waist. They inched forward together, slowly. 'I'd be better going down on my bottom,' Carrie announced cheerfully. 'Only I'm wearing these white shorts and Mum would murder me!'

'We can't see from up here, but there's a little sandy cove set back into the rock,' Jenny said, as they got nearer to the beach. 'He might be under the cliff, over towards the left.'

'Yes,' David agreed. 'I discovered that with my dad last week.'

'You know loads about Cliffbay already,' Fiona said, as she and Carrie caught up.

'My dad and I have been up here a lot since we came. Exploring,' David explained.

'Does your dad work in Cliffbay?' Jenny asked, hoping her feet were not going to slide from under her and send her crashing into David's back.

'Oh, er, sort of,' David said. 'He's always busy . . . Look, here's the beach. We're almost down.'

As soon as Jenny's feet touched the beach she sprinted forward, shouting for Jess.

Orla bounded alongside her, keen for a game. The sea was pounding into the shore and dragging itself back again noisily. Orla suddenly stopped scampering about excitedly and stood quite still. Her ears pricked and she lifted one paw, looking hard into the distance. Jenny followed her gaze and saw a dark speck over near the cliff. Orla's nose quivered. Then she barked sharply and set off at top speed.

'There!' David said with satisfaction. 'Orla's found him. I'll bet she has.'

'I can't see anything,' Fiona said.

'Neither can I,' Carrie agreed.

Jenny began to run on ahead, wishing she had worn her trainers instead of sandals. The wind whipped her hair across her face, making it difficult to see. She was beginning to think that Jess must have hurt himself. That would explain his absence. She ran faster.

Jess yapped excitedly when he saw Jenny coming. At his feet Jenny could see a dark shape, bulky in outline and about the size of a man's boot. Orla, streaking ahead of her, reached Jess first. Her tail was rigid as she stalked up to the strange dog and sniffed him all over. Then, she relaxed and her tail began to wag. Jess wagged his tail, too, but he didn't move. It looked to Jenny as though Jess was guarding something.

Jenny slowed to a walk. Her heart was thumping from her effort. 'Jess! What is it?' she shouted. Still Jess didn't move.

'He's not hurt, is he?' panted David, jogging up beside Jenny.

'No,' Jenny frowned in concern. 'It's just that he won't leave that spot. He seems to be guarding something. That must be the reason. He's never disobedient.'

They covered the last few metres together. Jess's

tail thumped harder as Jenny approached. 'Oh, Jess!' Jenny began. 'What have you got there?' A large bird was lying on the sand between Jess's front paws. Jenny's hand flew to her nose. The smell that came off it was powerful and turned her stomach. A big wave came thrashing up the beach and rolled the bird around. Jess put his paw onto its dead body and held it firmly.

'Look!' Jenny said urgently. 'Jess wants us to see what he's found. It's a dead puffin . . . and it's covered in something!' She kneeled in the sand and peered at the poor bird. 'Oh, no! It's oil!' she exclaimed. Jess lifted his paw and nudged it gently towards her.

'Yes, Jess,' she told him gently. 'I can see it. Good boy.'

'What is it?' Carrie asked, arriving with Fiona.

'A puffin, coated in black oil,' David told them. 'It's dead.' Jess looked down at the bird and barked. Orla barked in reply. David walked off towards the tide line.

'Oh, gosh,' Carrie put her hand to her mouth.

'What a pity,' Fiona said, sadly.

'It *is* oil!' David called to the girls. 'It's lapping along the edge of the beach.'

Carrie looked at Jenny, who looked at Fiona. 'There must have been an oil spill from a tanker somewhere up the coast. All the birds on Puffin Island might be in danger!' Carrie breathed.

'Jess was trying to warn us,' Jenny said, her eyes wide. 'That's why he wouldn't leave the bird. He wanted us to know what's happened.'

'Hadn't we better do something?' Fiona asked.

'Yes,' David said. 'We should go back to Cliffbay for help.'

'Let's go, then,' Jenny said. 'And quickly!'

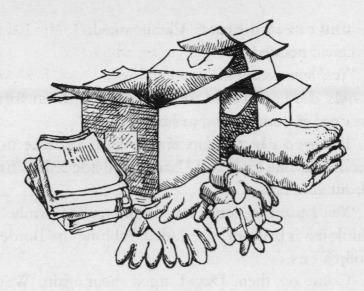

2

'Come on, Jess,' Jenny said, stroking his head. Jess put his nose into the palm of Jenny's hand. His tail thumped rhythmically against her leg. 'Well done – you're a clever boy.'

'Come on.' David was agitated. 'Let's get moving.' He looked at Carrie, who had sat down on the beach. Wearily, she got up. 'My dad's got a motor-boat,' he went on. 'I'll ask him if he'll take me out to the island to check if there are any birds in trouble. We could all go, if you like.' He looked a bit shy.

'Out to Puffin Island?' Carrie asked.

David nodded.

'Yes,' Jenny smiled.

'My dad's got a boat too,' Carrie told David. 'But he's not at home today, so he can't help.'

'But we'd like to help, if your dad will take us,' Jenny said. She looked at Carrie, who nodded. 'What about you, Fiona?'

'Yes, I want to come too,' Fiona replied firmly. 'I think Jess is brilliant,' she added, rubbing the Border collie's ears.

'Come on, then,' David urged them again. 'We'd better hurry.'

The wind whipped at their clothing as they walked back across the beach. They went in the opposite direction to the cliff path, heading quickly for the fishing village of Cliffbay, at the heart of which lay a small harbour. Jess and Orla ran ahead.

Carrie seemed to be struggling to keep up with the others. She was out of breath again. 'I told my mum I was just going out for a short walk with you, Fiona and Jess,' she gasped to Jenny. 'If we do go out on David's father's boat, I'll have to ring her and let her know.'

'There's the public call box,' Fiona said, pointing,

as they reached the crest of the hill at the harbour wall. 'Shall we ring the coastguard and tell them what we've found first?'

'Yes, the sooner the better,' Jenny agreed. 'Who's got some coins?'

'Me,' Carrie said.

'You won't need any money,' Fiona told her, holding the door open. 'Those sort of important numbers don't cost anything.'

On the wall inside the phone box was a list of emergency services that could be contacted free when you dialled 999. Jenny checked quickly and, under Police and Ambulance, she found Coastguard.

She held the black receiver to her ear and waited impatiently to be put through.

Outside the phone booth, Jess was getting to know Orla. They were walking around each other, sizing one another up, doing a lot of sniffing and tail-wagging. David was sitting astride a low wall, re-tying his shoelaces.

The phone at the other end was picked up.

'Hello?' Jenny said into the receiver. 'Is that the coastguard? Oh . . . he's busy is he?' Jenny made an exasperated face at Fiona and Carrie, who were listening at the door of the phone box. 'A message? Um, yes, please, well, I just wanted to report that I'd seen oil on the beach at Cliffbay today, you see . . . Oh, you know about it! Oh, that sounds bad. Yes, OK, thank you. Bye.'

'What did they say?' Carrie demanded.

David got down and came over. They huddled round Jenny.

'A tanker ship further up the coast *has* spilled its oil. They don't yet know how much but it seems fairly bad. They've already started trying to clean it up.' Jenny reported.

'Oh, that's awful,' Carrie said sadly.

'Wow,' said David. 'Let's go and see if we can help. If that puffin we found had oil on it, then it must be spreading quickly down the coast.'

'It's not only the birds who'll suffer,' Fiona said. 'What about the fish, and the shellfish and things . . .' she trailed off.

'I'll try Mr Palmer, the vet, first,' Jenny said. 'He'll know what to do.' She found the surgery number in the phone book and dialled. The phone was picked up straight away.

'Palmer's Veterinary Surgery,' said a woman's voice. 'Good morning.'

'Hello?' Jenny said. 'Is Mr Palmer there, please? This is Jenny Miles speaking.'

'Hello.' The receptionist's voice was friendly. 'I'm afraid Mr Palmer isn't here at the moment, Jenny. He's been called out. Is there a message?'

'No, it's all right. Thank you,' Jenny said.

'Have you a problem?' the voice asked.

'No, no problem. It's just that I . . . we . . . found a dead bird on the beach covered in oil. I wanted to tell him about it,' Jenny said.

'Ah, yes,' the receptionist said. 'We know about the oil spill. In fact, Mr Palmer has gone out to investigate the situation. But thank you for the information. I'll pass it on, all right?'

'OK, thanks. Bye.'

'Bye, Jenny.' The phone went dead. She stepped

out of the phone box and faced the others.

'What is it?' Carrie said. 'Any news?'

'Tom Palmer isn't at the surgery today – he's been called away – to help the birds, the lady said.'

'Well, let's go then, shall we?' David urged.

'I'll just ring my mum,' Carrie said, feeling in her shorts pocket for a coin. She went into the phone box.

'My house is only a few minutes walk from here,' David said. We can give the dogs a drink and leave them there, if you want. Orla doesn't like going in the boat,' he added.

'Jess does,' Jenny said firmly. 'He'll come with me.' Jenny smoothed Jess's silky ears. He was panting and his tongue looked dry. The sooner they got to David's house, the better.

'Mum says it's OK to go to Puffin Island,' Carrie said, coming out of the phone box. 'She knows about the spill. It's been on the local news. Apparently, everyone's rushing about trying to help.'

'Right, then,' said David, bending to clip on Orla's lead. 'Follow me.'

Fiona hurried after David and Carrie followed more slowly behind. Jess was already waiting at Jenny's side. 'Come on, boy,' she said. 'Let's catch up with Carrie.'

★　★　★

David's house was a whitewashed bungalow with a carefully kept, rectangular garden. It was partly fenced, but in places the fence had fallen down and was in the process of being mended. Jenny had noticed the place before, when it had been empty and its garden hopelessly overgrown. Now, patterned curtains fluttered at the open windows and the flower borders were a riot of colour. She and Jess, with Carrie and Fiona, followed David and Orla up to the front door.

'Um, can you wait out here?' David said uncomfortably, not looking at them.' I'll go and find my dad.'

Jenny exchanged looks with Carrie and Fiona. She thought it was a bit odd of David not to invite them in but, noticing that Carrie still looked a bit washed out and would probably be grateful of a rest, she turned towards the garden.

'Let's sit over there,' she said, pointing to a patch of grass.

Carrie gave a long sigh.'Phew! It's hot,' she smiled.

'Nice garden,' Fiona commented, looking around.

Jess lay down on the manicured lawn. He was still panting but his eyes were bright and alert. Jenny guessed that he knew something was up and was enjoying being involved.

'Isn't it funny that David made us wait out here?' Carrie whispered, frowning suspiciously at the front door. 'Why do you think he didn't want us to go inside with him?'

'Maybe he's got something to hide . . .' Fiona suggested.

'Oh, I'm sure!' Carrie teased. 'He and his dad are probably smugglers . . .'

At that moment, the front door of the house opened and David came out, carefully carrying a plastic bowl of water for Jess. The collie ran to David, lifting his nose eagerly to the cold, fresh water.

'Thanks,' Jenny said, as Jess began to lap thirstily.

'My dad's been on the phone to the SSPCA,' David told them. 'They've agreed to send someone over to Puffin Island as soon as they can but, right now, they're all very busy up the main spill higher up the coast. Even the Puffin Island warden has gone out there. Dad'll take us over to the island – he says they're glad of all the help they can get.'

'Great.' Jenny got to her feet just as Jess barked sharply once, as a man appeared in the doorway of the bungalow.

'Good afternoon!' He had a booming voice. 'I'm John Fergusson, David's father.'

'Thanks for taking us out to the island, Mr Fergusson,' Jenny said. 'I'm Jenny Miles. These are my friends Carrie Turner and Fiona McLay.' Carrie and Fiona said hello, together.

Mr Fergusson was a tall, thin man with grey hair. He wore a yellow waterproof jacket. 'Good sailors, are you?' he asked.

'Yes, I am,' Carrie answered. 'I often go out in my dad's boat. He runs trips to Puffin Island in the summer.'

'I'm not bad either,' Fiona said.

'I'm OK,' Jenny added.

'Right. Sounds like the birds on the island might need help,' Mr Fergusson said. 'Sad business. Let's go then, shall we? That dog coming too?'

'Yes,' Jenny spoke up. 'This is Jess. He'll come . . . that is, if you don't mind.'

'Not at all,' said Mr Fergusson, as he led the way to his garage.

The boat was a sleek and powerful craft, called *Hadrian*. With the help of the others, Mr Fergusson jammed every available bit of space with the equipment they would need for the rescue of wild seabirds. He packed a heap of stacked cardboard boxes, a pile of old newspapers, a blanket or two, and an assortment of gloves – from rubber gloves to thick fabric gardening gloves and some woolly winter mittens.

Jess jumped into the boat, finding a narrow space to sit down at Jenny's feet. She sat squeezed up next to Carrie, who was beside Fiona. David sat with his father in the front of the boat.

'Remember,' Mr Fergusson warned, 'these birds may bite, so don't think you can just pluck them off the beach without protecting your hands, OK? Also, oil is toxic. If you get some on your hands, don't put them near your eyes or mouth.'

'Absolutely not,' Carrie grinned, looking in mock horror at her fingers.

Jess put his front feet up onto the edge of Jenny's seat and looked out as they headed towards the open sea. The wind blew his ears flat on the top of his head. He lifted his nose to the sea air and wagged his tail.

'You OK with Jess back there?' Mr Fergusson shouted, gripping the wheel.

'Fine,' Jenny shouted in reply, though the wind seemed to whip the words right out of her mouth and throw them into the air. She was beginning to wish that she had followed Carrie's example and rung home to let Ellen Grace know what was happening.

'OK?' Carrie asked her, as Jenny frowned.

'I should have phoned to say where I was going, like you did,' Jenny admitted.

'Don't worry, Jen,' Carrie said. 'If Mrs Grace worries about you, she'll ring my mum, you know she will.'

'Yes, you're right,' Jenny said, smiling at her friend.

Mr Fergusson eased the boat to the left and, ahead of them, they could see the shadowy outline of Puffin Island in the distance. The cloud was low and the wind was churning up little white waves across the sea. The boat slapped against the water. Jess got a mouthful of salty spray. He sneezed violently. Everyone laughed.

'Oh, poor Jess,' Jenny said, putting her arm round him to steady him as he tried to wipe at his eyes with one paw.

'Are you girls pupils at Greybridge?' Mr Fergusson asked, half turning so they could hear him in the back.

'Yes, we are,' Jenny replied.

'Fortunate for David, then, that you met before school starts. Good to know a few faces in a new place,' he said.

'Do you like Cliffbay, Mr Fergusson?' Jenny asked.

'So far,' he said cautiously. 'I'm a keen

conservationist and I like birds. So Cliffbay will do nicely.'

'Where did you live before you came here?' Fiona yelled, to make herself heard.

John Fergusson looked at his son, then half turned to look at Fiona. 'Different places,' he replied. 'All over.'

Fiona glanced at Jenny, who shrugged. It seemed difficult to get any straight answers out of either David or his father. Jenny was beginning to find them both a bit mysterious.

'Nearly there!' said David. The island was right ahead of them now. It was a rocky outcrop with just a few trees and a shingle beach sloping down to the sea. Mr Fergusson slowed *Hadrian*'s engine and they eased in closer to shore.

'Oh . . . look!' said Jenny. David stood up and looked out. The sea lapping against the island had streaks of oil on it. Slicks of oil rode on the water in patches.

'Oh, no,' Carrie breathed. 'The poor puffins!'

'I can't bear it,' Fiona said, in a small voice.

'The slick is drifting in from the east – and Puffin Island is right in its path,' Mr Fergusson reported, shaking his head. He switched off the boat's engine and let the tide take him in.

'There's a harbour round the other side of the island,' Carrie told him.

'This will be quicker,' Mr Fergusson assured her.

David jumped out and hauled the keel up over the stones. It made a grating noise that sent shivers up Jenny's spine. As she got to her feet, Jess jumped over the side of the boat. He landed in the shallow water then bounded excitedly up the beach.

Jenny leaped out and looked around her. It was a pitiful sight. Already some of the birds had fallen victim to the oil snaking up the beach. A few puffins, their pale grey and white feathered chests coated in black oil, were struggling around in panic. Even the colourful stripes of their beaks were covered.

She recognised some sleek, fat, white bodies as gulls, and gannets – with their dagger-shaped beaks opening and closing soundlessly and their big black feet slapping around in bewilderment on the oily beach. Black guillemots were bunched together miserably, too weary from their struggle even to move away from the strangers who had arrived in their haven. One was walking round in a circle, dragging its wing.

'Mr Fergusson!' Jenny shouted. 'What can we do to help?' But Mr Fergusson was striding away to inspect the extent of the damage and didn't reply.

Carrie and Fiona stood beside her.

'Look,' David pointed. 'A grey plover. It's dead.'

The bird lay at David's feet. A swirl of oil came up the beach in a rush of sea. When the sea drew back, it left its ugly mark on a patch of pale gold stone.

'Oh, poor thing!' said Carrie.

Fiona peered at the bird. 'How horrible,' she said sadly.

'Let's unload those boxes and things,' Jenny said urgently. 'There are live birds that need our help! Now!'

3

David clambered aboard *Hadrian*. Already his jeans were wet up to the knees but Jenny was relieved to see that he didn't seem to mind, or even to notice. He seemed as determined as she felt to help the birds.

Jenny, Fiona and Carrie stood in a line below the hull of the boat, reaching up for the boxes, blankets, gloves and newspapers that David unloaded. Jess stood watching the operation with interest.

'You're doing a great job,' announced Mr

Fergusson, striding back towards the boat. 'Let's get everything out of the boat and away from the water.' He stooped to lift their supplies out of the hull and take them higher up the beach. Jess picked up a glove, and followed him, dropping it helpfully at his feet. 'Good boy!' David's father said approvingly. 'I trust Jess will behave himself? He won't worry the birds?' he asked Jenny.

'No way!' Fiona said, loyally.

'He's a sheepdog,' Jenny explained. 'Even though he's not really a working dog, he's got good instincts. As well as that, his nature is gentle and caring.' She felt proud of the Border collie. 'We strapped bottles of milk to him once, to get the feed out to the weaker of the orphaned lambs in the fields. He did a brilliant job of being a surrogate mum.' She felt certain Jess wouldn't harm the birds, some of which were now battling for their lives.

'Where do we begin?' Carrie asked, dusting the fine sand off her palms. Jenny, too, was impatient to start.

'By lining the cardboard boxes with newspaper to provide warmth,' Mr Fergusson advised. 'Then, go round the island picking up the birds, gently and carefully, from behind. Put them into the boxes as quickly as you can. Most boxes will take at least two birds, some will take three. Close the lids to make it as dark as possible.'

'Why?' Jenny asked. 'I mean, why does it have to be dark?'

'So they won't be scared?' Fiona suggested.

'Well, yes, but mainly it helps to stop them trying to preen the oil off their feathers. It's toxic and if they swallow it, it'll kill them,' he explained. 'Generally, they don't preen themselves in the dark.'

David handed round the boxes while his father talked. He was frowning with concentration, working quickly. Jenny, Carrie and Fiona began stuffing the newspapers into them.

'Right,' Mr Fergusson went on. 'Let me give you a few more pointers. The birds needing help will be found above the strand line, all the way round the island. They will have been washed in from the sea during high tide, early this morning.'

'There are still some birds out at sea,' Fiona noticed, pointing.

Mr Fergusson nodded. 'The ones that have come into shore have done so because they can't stay afloat,' Mr Fergusson explained. 'The oil removes the waterproofing on their feathers. If they stayed out in the water, they would drown. With oil on their wings, they are unable to fly, either. In this situation they

31

only leave the sea when they're really desperate. The water is their natural habitat and where they feel safest.'

'Oh, poor things,' said Carrie.

'Your father seem to know a lot about saving birds,' Jenny whispered to David.

'He once worked as a volunteer for a wildlife hospital,' David explained, as he tore newspaper into strips to fit it snugly into a small box.

'So, they only come ashore when they're in *real* trouble?' Fiona asked.

'That's right,' Mr Fergusson replied. He passed round the gloves. Jenny was given a thick pair of gardening gloves. They were huge. She wondered how she was going to keep them on her hands.

'Now,' Mr Fergusson said, 'we'll take as many birds as we can, OK? Bring the boxes back to the boat when they're full. It's probably going to be necessary to make a second trip to the island, once we've got the first lot back to the mainland.'

Jenny picked up two of the lined boxes. She looked at Jess, who looked back at her.

'Stay, Jess,' Jenny said. The collie lay down and put his nose on his paws and gave a little sigh.

'Good boy,' Jenny told him. 'You know it's best if you wait here, don't you?' Quickly, she bent to stroke his silky head and Jess stayed perfectly still. Jenny smiled. Her father was always amazed at the way the young Border collie was so perfectly in tune with what she expected of him. Jenny never doubted Jess for a moment.

She looked around her. Carrie and Fiona were following Mr Fergusson across the beach. David had gone off round the island in the opposite direction. Wanting to make sure she gathered up her first wild seabird in the correct way, Jenny decided to stick close to Mr Fergusson. He seemed to be an expert at these things. She ran to catch up.

'It's a razorbill,' Mr Fergusson was saying, as Jenny drew close. He was looking at a bird on the shingle. The seabird's wings were spread stiffly and it blinked small eyes covered in oil.

'Poor old thing,' Mr Fergusson said, as he crouched and crept towards it, then made a swift grab from behind. The bird squawked. Mr Fergusson held it firmly but gently between the palms of his gloved hands. It twisted its neck, trying to sink its beak into his fingers. Jenny's heart turned over for the poor, terrified creature. Mr Fergusson plunged it down into the box and secured the cardboard flaps over its head.

'I can do that!' Carrie said. 'Nothing to it.' She grinned at Jenny, who gave her a watery smile. Carrie was always so positive and cheerful, but that was far from the way Jenny was feeling right at this moment. She looked at her hands, thinking about how determined the bird had been to bite.

'There,' Mr Fergusson straightened. 'There's room for a couple more birds in this box, so . . . off you go. Get busy!' he said firmly, clapping his hands playfully. Jenny started.

'Right,' she said. 'Right, Mr Fergusson.' She looked longingly after Carrie, as she wandered away with her boxes, wishing that they could work as a team. She loved Carrie's sparky company and had missed her while she was ill at home. But, she reasoned to herself, there were only five of them, and many more birds needing to be discovered and helped. She picked up her boxes. Fiona picked up hers.

'Let's spread out, then,' Jenny said.

'Yes,' Fiona agreed, and headed towards the summit of Puffin Island.

Jenny spotted a small gull hunched miserably on a stone. It was shaking its small head, which was covered in oil. She began nervously to sneak up on it. The bird made no attempt to fly off, even though her sandals crunched noisily on the shingle as she approached.

The gull felt light in her hands. The wings were

thick with oozing black oil that coated the gloves and seeped through to Jenny's fingers. In spite of the gloves being so hefty, and so big for her, she was glad she had them on. Mr Fergusson had said that this foul-smelling oil was poisonous for the birds – what harm might it do to her if she got it on her skin, she wondered? She laid the bird gently in the box. As she closed the lid, the oil from her gloves smeared across the flaps.

'Ugh!' she said, making a face as David came up. 'This is disgusting.'

David was holding a large cardboard box against his chest. 'I've got three birds in mine,' he told her. 'They're crammed in pretty tight, poor things. Have you been over on the other side, by the rocks? There are loads there.'

'No,' Jenny said. 'I'll have a look now.' She carried the gull carefully, hating the feel of the small, sharp stones and the slimy oil that came in through the sides of her sandals. She guessed she would have to throw them away when she got home.

'You coping?' called Mr Fergusson, struggling with a frantic gannet.

'Um, yes,' Jenny replied. 'This is awful, isn't it?'

'Not as bad as it might be,' he said gravely. 'I've seen worse. Puffin Island hasn't been badly affected, luckily. The slick is further up the coast. Who knows what damage it might do up there.'

'Can they scoop it out of the sea?' Jenny asked, adding, in a sudden spark of anger: 'They should make the people responsible for spilling it clean it up!'

'They try and disperse it with chemicals,' Mr Fergusson said, shaking his head. 'But oil slicks do a lot of damage the moment they hit. Everything in the sea, from periwinkles to shrimps, anemones and even rare sea grasses, could be wiped out by a big spill of crude oil. But . . .' he sighed, 'we have to hope for the best.'

Jenny looked out across the sea. She imagined the oil, as thick as chocolate, spreading slowly towards the little island, and the birds, opening and shutting their beaks, as if calling for help. Her eyes stung with tears.

Carrie passed by with a box pressed against her thighs. The lid was lifting as the bird inside struggled to be free. 'I've got a cross one in here, Mr Fergusson,' she called.

Jenny noticed that Carrie looked exhausted. Her face was as white as a sheet and there were shadows like bruises under her eyes.

'It should settle down in a minute or two,' Mr

Fergusson called after her. 'But I'd put a stone on the top of the box.'

Jenny hurriedly scooped another stricken bird off the beach and put it in with her gull, then caught up with Carrie, who was on her way back to where *Hadrian* was moored.

'I'm tired,' Carrie announced. 'I think I'll get on the boat and have a little rest.'

'Oh,' Jenny said, disappointed. 'It's not like you to give up so soon. We're doing such a good job.'

'I just want to sit down for a bit. I won't be long,' Carrie replied.

'But these birds need our help now!' Jenny said heatedly. 'Otherwise they may die!'

Carrie let out a sigh. 'OK! All right, Jenny. You win. Honestly, you're such a nag at times,' she said.

'I am not!' Jenny returned, feeling hurt. Carrie wasn't behaving like her usual self at all.

'It's quite easy to catch them, isn't it?' Fiona said, as Jenny and Carrie came up to the boat.

The interruption put an end to the argument. Jenny nodded and smiled weakly at Fiona. She suddenly felt embarrassed about the way she had reacted to Carrie. She had got caught up in the momentum of the rescue and, forgetting Carrie was ill, felt annoyed that she wasn't her usual enthusiastic

37

self. It wasn't like her friend just to give up on something because she felt like it.

When Jess spotted Jenny, he stood up and wagged his tail hard. She called to him and he bounded over joyfully, lifting his nose to sniff at the box she was carrying. She laid it down beside Carrie's and Fiona's, then made a fuss of him.

Carrie put a large stone on the lid of her box. 'I'm going back to look for more birds,' she said, in a determined voice.

'That's the spirit,' Jenny teased. But Carrie didn't turn round and make a funny face at her as Jenny had thought she would. She just walked away.

'I think we've got enough to make a first trip back now,' Mr Fergusson decided, as he added his box to the row. 'We'd better start loading them aboard.'

'Oh, but I haven't filled my second box yet!' Jenny pleaded.

'All right, Jenny. 'Go and see what you can find as quickly as you can. OK?' Mr Fergusson said.

'Wait here for me, Jess,' Jenny said urgently and ran down the beach with her box. She decided to head towards the rocks where Carrie was going. There were bound to be plenty of seabirds trying to take shelter there. She slowed to a jog, feeling her legs begin to ache with tiredness. It had been a long day. She would give anything to stop and have a cold drink.

Ahead of her, she could see Carrie on the rocks. Her friend was feeling her way carefully – trying – Jenny guessed, not to slip on the oil. She hoped Carrie wasn't annoyed with her. She hadn't meant to sound like an old nag. When she caught up with her, Jenny decided, she would say she was sorry.

She saw Carrie spread out her arms, as if for better balance. Then, suddenly, she disappeared from Jenny's view. One moment she was there, and the next, she wasn't. She waited to see if Carrie would appear again, but she didn't. Her heart began to hammer in her chest.

'Carrie!' Jenny shouted and started to run towards the rocks. 'Where are you?' She looked back for somebody who would help. Mr Fergusson . . . David . . . Fiona? But they were aboard *Hadrian*, engrossed in stacking the birds.

Jenny reached the rocks. She slowed and stepped cautiously onto the jagged surface, slimy with thick, black oil. There were pools of it forming in the crevices. She put out her arms for better balance and stared around her.

Carrie was lying face down. The oily sea licked at

her outstretched arm. 'Carrie!' Jenny screamed. But Carrie didn't move.

Stumbling and sliding, Jenny went towards her friend. The sea rushed in to cover the rocks, making it impossible for Jenny to see where next to step. She paused, her heart pounding so hard she could hear it. Carrie hadn't moved, in spite of the cold water splashing up against her, touching her with the oil. *Could she have struck her head when she fell? Might she drown?* Jenny thought frantically.

'Carrie!' she shrieked again. She couldn't move any faster. The waves on the rocks and the oil made it too dangerous to hurry. Then, suddenly, Jenny heard a welcome sound. She looked up.

Jess was flying across the beach towards her. His ears were up and his tail streamed out behind him in the wind. He was barking as he ran.

'Jess! Oh, Jess,' sobbed Jenny. 'Good boy! Come, come quickly . . .'

Jess must have sensed by the tone of her voice as she called to Carrie that something was wrong. Now, he sprang onto the rocks, his claws gripping where Jenny's sandals wouldn't hold. He found a passage towards her. Jenny's heart nearly stopped beating when she saw him stagger under a powerful wave. Then he was beside her. She pulled off her glove and stroked his head gratefully.

'Jess,' she told him firmly. 'Go and get help. Get Mr Fergusson, or David . . . or Fiona. Good boy! Go!' Jess put his head to one side, listening. He looked first to where Jenny was pointing back at the beach, then back at her face. 'Quick, Jess!' Jenny said again.

Jess sprang off the rocks and ran back towards the boat. In the distance, Jenny could see Mr Fergusson jump from the deck of *Hadrian* onto the beach. He stooped to roll up his trouser legs. Jenny saw him look up as the wet, oily dog came streaking towards him. He straightened up. Jess let out a volley of sharp barks, then turned and ran back towards the rocks.

Mr Fergusson put up a hand to shade his eyes from the glare and peered in the direction the dog was running. Jenny waved her arms frantically and a few seconds later he caught sight of her, waved back, and then began to run.

'What is it?' he shouted as he got nearer.

'It's Carrie,' Jenny yelled back. 'My friend . . . she's unconscious. You've got to help her, please!'

4

Jenny felt the relief surge through her. Help was on the way. As the next wave pulled back off the rocks, she quickly covered the last couple of metres to where Carrie was lying. She was surprised to find her friend curled up on her side, looking quite peaceful, as though she had chosen this spot to have a sleep.

Jenny bent down and put a hand on her shoulder. 'Carrie!' she said, urgently. 'Carrie . . . are you all right?' Carrie's eyelids fluttered and she gave a small groan.

'What's happened?' Mr Fergusson was out of breath from his dash down the beach. His voice was gruff with alarm. He was staggering around on the rocks, trying to keep his balance and peer at Carrie at the same time. Jess stood firm, gripping the rocks with his claws, his tail still and his ears flat. He whimpered.

'I think . . . well, she just fell down,' Jenny said, miserably. 'I don't know what happened – if she collapsed, or just slipped.'

'What's the matter?' Fiona shouted, from the beach.

'Stay where you are,' Mr Fergusson ordered Fiona. 'You and David keep an eye on the birds.' He lifted Carrie, who slumped against him, just as a large wave came swooshing up the rocks, showering them both with cold water.

Carrie coughed, then blinked and opened her eyes. She looked at Jenny's worried face, and frowned with confusion, as if trying to remember where she was. 'Sorry,' she said, shyly, as Mr Fergusson pulled her to her feet. 'I took a tumble . . . tripped, or something.'

'Oh, Carrie!' Jenny breathed. 'You gave me such a fright! How do you feel?'

'Well, that wasn't the most comfortable bed!' Carrie said, sounding more like her old self. 'But I'm OK.' She looked down at her legs, which were covered in cuts and scratches. Jess put his nose gently into the palm of Carrie's hand.

'Hello, Jess. Yes, I'm all right now.' Carrie managed a giggle as Jess's tongue darted out to lick at her bare legs. They were caked with salt and traced with blood. Her white shorts were ripped and streaked with oil.

'It was the dog who let me know something was up,' Mr Fergusson said, admiringly. 'He's an intelligent animal, I'll say that.' Jenny put her hand out to Jess and stroked him proudly.

Mr Fergusson kept a firm hold on Carrie's upper arm as he helped her off the rocks. Then Jenny slipped her arm round Carrie's waist and walked with her up the beach back to the boat. She was trembling all over and Carrie laughed.

'You're shaking like a jelly in a high wind, Jen. It's *me* who should be doing the shaking!'

Jenny was overcome with relief that her best friend was safe. She felt awful for having spoken sharply to Carrie earlier. 'Are you OK? I mean, *really* OK?' she asked quietly.

'Fine,' Carrie replied. 'Now, stop fussing. I tripped, that's all. I must have banged my head or something. It's nothing. Oh, hello, Fiona . . .'

'Oh, your legs!' Fiona gasped, seeing a trickle of blood snaking down Carrie's calf. 'Did you fall?'

'Yep,' Carrie said cheerfully. 'Tripped over a wave.' She chuckled, but Jenny noticed that she was still very pale.

'Right,' said Mr Fergusson, 'Let's have you all in the boat now and we'll head for the mainland. I want to get these birds to the vet.'

Every centimetre of *Hadrian*'s hull was occupied by boxes containing birds. Jenny, Carrie and Fiona were crushed into the back of the boat, Jess at their feet. Their laps were laden with boxes, some unmoving, some being buffeted by the bewildered creatures inside. David had several boxes at the front with him. As Mr Fergusson opened the throttle and

headed back to Cliffbay, Carrie quietly laid her head against Jenny's shoulder and closed her eyes.

Jenny tried not to mind about being so wet and uncomfortable. She'd noticed her toe was bleeding, too, and now it began to sting. But they'd rescued, and probably saved, a good number of seabirds – and Carrie was safe beside her. That was all that mattered.

She put out her hand and her fingers found the fur of Jess's soft chest. She began to tickle and scratch him and in return he licked her hand lovingly. 'Nearly home,' she whispered. 'And, do *you* deserve a treat!'

When *Hadrian* was secured at her mooring, Mr Fergusson transferred the birds to the back of his van. 'I'll take you straight home, young lady,' he said to Carrie, climbing into the cab. 'Then we must hurry these birds to a vet. They'll be needing treatment as soon as possible.'

'What sort of treatment, Mr Fergusson?' Fiona asked.

'They need to drink,' he told her. 'They'll be dehydrated, and also very cold. They need rehydration and a heat lamp, or a warm room in which to recover.'

'Will you be going back to Puffin Island for more birds, Dad?' David asked.

'We'll see. One of the specialist agencies should be on the job pretty soon,' Mr Fergusson replied. 'They may not need our help.'

Carrie seemed to doze off again as they drove, saying nothing when Jenny gave David's father instructions on how to find the Turners' home. She sat up just as they arrived at Cliff House, and Mr Fergusson pulled up beside Mrs Turner's brightly painted mini.

Carrie opened the door of the van. 'Thanks, Mr Fergusson, bye everyone,' she said with a smile.

Jenny moved to climb out. 'I'll come in with you . . .' she began.

'No,' Carrie spoke firmly. 'No you won't. Those birds in the back need your help. My mum's here for me.'

'But . . . you're not well,' Jenny said.

Carrie pushed her coppery hair out of her eyes and straightened her shoulders. 'Go to Mr Palmer's surgery!' she pleaded. 'I'm *fine*.' She guided Jenny back into the van and closed the door. Then she stood back and waved as Mr Fergusson pulled away.

Jenny craned her neck to look back at Carrie. Mrs Turner had come out of the house. The warm smile of greeting vanished from her face when she saw the state of her daughter. She put her arms round Carrie who, in turn, buried her face in her mother's shoulder. As they drove away down the street and Jenny lost sight of them, she didn't know why – but she just couldn't shake off a feeling of real worry for her friend.

Tom Palmer, the vet, was a big man with a loud voice, but Jenny had always liked him. It had been Mr Palmer who had given Jess the chance to lead a normal life. He had performed the operation that had straightened out the puppy's crippled leg. Over the months, Jess's leg had got progressively stronger, so that now, the slight limp he had had since being a pup was barely noticeable.

'Jenny!' Mr Palmer beamed, and removed the stethoscope that was swinging from his neck. 'How nice to see you. How are you?'

'Hello, Mr Palmer.' Jenny smiled. 'I'm fine, thanks,' she replied, despite the fact that she was feeling so tired she was almost seeing double and her stomach was growling with hunger. 'This is Mr Fergusson. He took us out to the island and we helped him to rescue some seabirds that . . .'

'The birds are in the back of the van,' Mr Fergusson

said hurriedly, interrupting Jenny. 'They need seeing to, and pretty quick I'd say.'

'Ah, yes,' Tom Palmer frowned. 'Nasty business. It was a South American oil tanker, I believe. I've been told its engines failed, and the ship was dragged round by the tide onto some rocks. The hull split open.'

'What happened to the people on the ship?' David asked, his eyes wide.

'They're being taken off by the lifeboats,' Mr Palmer said. 'We're hoping the full might of the slick doesn't move this way, though there is bound to be some damage.'

'It was Jess who discovered an oil-covered puffin on the beach at Cliffbay this morning,' Jenny told him. 'So really it's him who let us know about the spill and made us go out to the island to see if we could help.'

'Ah, a fine young dog, is that Jess,' smiled Tom Palmer. 'Where is he, by the way?'

'He's out in the van,' Fiona said. 'He's been brilliant.'

'What about these birds, then?' David's father asked.

'Bring them in, Mr Fergusson, if you don't mind. And, well done – all of you.' Mr Palmer smiled, putting a gentle hand on Jenny's tousled head. 'From the look of you, it's been a long, hard day.'

David followed his father out of the surgery. Fiona trailed wearily in their wake. 'Let Jess in, too, lass,' Mr Palmer said kindly, to Jenny. 'He'll be needing a drink, I'll bet.'

'Thanks.' Jenny grinned and then ran to release Jess from the back of the van and bring him inside.

A room had been given over to the emergency treatment of wildlife that had suffered from the oil spill. To Jenny's amazement, even a small seal pup was snoozing under a lamp. Tom Palmer and his two assistants had used all the available equipment to heat the room. Makeshift barricades had become holding pens for an assortment of sea creatures. Heat lamps shone their eerie red glow onto shivering birds.

Jess, with water dripping from his muzzle, walked about peering into the pens, his nose twitching with the smell of the oil.

'What a hero, you are, young Jess!' said Mr Palmer, patting his side. Jess's tail thumped happily on the floor.

Mr Palmer handed out gloves to everyone and they helped him to put the birds into the appropriate pens. 'My,' he said admiringly, 'you've done a good job here. These birds would certainly have died if you hadn't been there to help.'

Jenny grinned at Fiona, who grinned back.

'What will happen to the birds now, Mr Palmer?' Fiona asked.

'They'll need about twenty-four hours to rehydrate and to get warm,' he told her. 'Then, those that live will be taken to the special centre run by the SSPCA to be cleaned. We haven't got the equipment needed for that here, you see, and a new place has just been opened in Graston.'

'Oh, yes, I read about that in the paper,' Jenny said. 'But shouldn't all that horrible oil be washed off straight away?'

'No,' Mr Palmer assured her. 'Being cold and thirsty will kill a bird more quickly than the oil will. This first step is vital for their survival. Someone will be coming along from the SSPCA to check on this latest lot in a minute, I expect.'

'No need for us to hang around, then?' Mr Fergusson said. 'It's been a long day.'

'No need at all, thank you. And I should think someone is on their way back to Puffin Island for more casualties even now.' Tom Palmer smiled. He reached down and smoothed Jess's coat. 'Good boy! A fine job . . .'

'I'll take you two home,' Mr Fergusson said to Jenny

and Fiona. 'Then I'm going to have a much needed cup of tea!'

'Thanks, Mr Fergusson,' Jenny said. She took a last look at the birds they had rescued. She hoped they *would* survive and that soon they would be released back to an oil-free Puffin Island. 'C'mon Jess,' Jenny called.

Fiona practically fell out of the van when they reached Dunraven, the McLays' home. She mumbled a goodbye to Jenny and David and thanked Mr Fergusson for the lift.

'See you, Fi,' Jenny said. Then she told David's father how to get to Windy Hill. Jess began to bark as they approached the farm gates.

'He wants his dinner!' David laughed.

'He's always pleased to be home.' Jenny smiled.

Fraser Miles was loading hay bales onto a tractor when Mr Fergusson's van pulled up. There were bits of straw in his dark hair and his wellington boots were caked in mud. He looked up and a grin spread across his face. 'Hello, love,' he said warmly, opening the door to let Jenny out. He ruffled Jess's ears as the collie came up to greet him. 'You look as though you've done three rounds in the ring with a champion boxer!'

'Oh, Dad, what a day we've had! We went out to Puffin Island with Mr Fergusson to save the birds from the oil . . .'

'How do you do?' Mr Miles said, putting out his hand. 'Thanks for bringing Jenny home. I heard from Ellen, who spoke to Mrs Turner, that you'd gone off on some adventure.'

'Hello,' Mr Fergusson took the outstretched hand. 'No problem.'

'I've heard about the oil spill. Nasty business. Did you save any birds then, Jen?' Fraser Miles asked with a grin.

'Yes, loads!' Jenny said proudly. 'Jess discovered a puffin covered in oil down on Cliffbay beach, so we knew there was a problem. Mr Fergusson took us out there in his motor-boat and showed us how to catch the birds. We've left the ones we rescued with Mr Palmer.'

'Well done, lass!' Jenny's dad said. 'You're new around here, aren't you?' he asked David's father.

'Yes, we moved in a week or so ago,' Mr Fergusson said. 'This is my son, David.' Fraser Miles nodded and smiled at David, who smiled back. 'We've taken a house at Cliffbay.'

'You're here on holiday here, then?' Mr Miles asked pleasantly.

'Uh . . . no, we're going to see how it goes . . .' he trailed off.

Fraser Miles looked puzzled. An awkward silence hung over them.

'Um, would you like a cup of tea, Mr Fergusson? David?' Jenny put in brightly, but hoping they would refuse. She was exhausted and desperate to get indoors to feed and groom Jess, and to have a shower. And now all the excitement was over, she realised how hungry she was.

'No, thanks,' said Mr Fergusson. 'We'll be off now. Nice to meet you.'

'See you at school, David,' Jenny said.

'Yes, on Monday.' He nodded.

'Thanks again,' Mr Miles said, as David and his father climbed into the van.

'By the way,' Mr Fergusson called, from the driver's window. 'That's a great dog you've got there.' Jess's tail thumped against Jenny's leg.

'Thanks!' she shouted, as the van drew away.

'There's something odd about Mr Fergusson,' Fraser Miles mused.

'Hmm, I think so too. But I can't think what it is,' Jenny agreed. She stretched and gave a sigh. *Perhaps Fiona is right*, she thought. *Perhaps we should be suspicious . . .*

But she was far too tired and hungry to give it much thought and calling Jess, Jenny gladly let herself into Windy Hill.

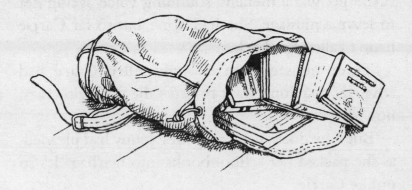

5

The moment Jenny arrived in her classroom on Monday morning her eyes wandered hopefully to Carrie's desk. She looked for the usual unruly head of red hair bent over a haphazard pile of books. But no laughing blue eyes looked back at her, and the desk itself was as neat as a pin.

Jenny sat down slowly at her own desk and gave a big sigh. She'd been trying to speak to Carrie since Mr Fergusson had dropped her home after the bird rescue three days ago. The Turners' had installed an answer machine on their telephone line and all Jenny could get was a metallic-sounding voice asking her to leave a message. She had done, but so far Carrie hadn't called her back.

'Three messages are enough,' Ellen Grace had advised. 'You don't want to drive the poor girl crazy, now do you?'

'But why doesn't she ring me?' Jenny had pleaded, as she packed her school books into her bag. 'It's so unlike Carrie.'

'I can't help you there, Jenny,' Mrs Grace had said kindly. 'Perhaps she's not well and her mother wants her to rest. That's simple enough, isn't it?'

'Yes, but usually Carrie would phone me back,' Jenny had said, feeling a bit hurt. 'I am her best friend, after all.'

Mrs Grace was wonderful, and had largely filled the enormous gap left in the heart of the family after Jenny's mother had died, but she didn't understand her in quite the way her mother had.

'No,' Jenny had insisted, 'I must've upset Carrie in some way. That's got to be the reason.'

'I'm sure you haven't, Jenny,' Ellen Grace had said, coming over to give Jenny a hug. 'Best friends are not that fragile. Especially not Carrie. She's a fighter, isn't that what you always told me?'

Yes, Jenny acknowledged to herself miserably, as she sat at her desk hoping Carrie's face would appear in the classroom doorway. *Carrie's a fighter, all right. So, where is she? What's happened to her?*

'Hello.'

Jenny jumped. David Fergusson stood there with his schoolbag over his shoulder, his dark hair neatly combed and flattened across his head. He looked different to the last time Jenny had seen him, with the wind whipping his hair round his face and the salt dried in patches on his cheeks.

'Hello,' she said brightly.

'Um, do you know where I should sit?' David asked, looking round awkwardly. 'I've been told to use Carrie Turner's desk for the day.'

'Oh!' Jenny started. 'Does that mean Carrie isn't coming in to school today?' She didn't know why she had asked him. Why would he have the answers that she didn't?

'I expect so . . .' David trailed off.

'It's this one,' Jenny said absently, pointing to the desk beside hers. She watched as David lifted the lid of the desk and look about inside, fitting his own few books in and around Carrie's.

'Where's Carrie?' Fiona asked, coming straight over from the doorway.

'Don't know,' Jenny mumbled. 'Sick, maybe?'

'I tried ringing her yesterday,' Fiona said. 'They've got an answer machine now.'

'Well,' David said, 'she did fall on the rocks, remember? Maybe she's not feeling too good because of that.'

Fiona perched on the edge of Jenny's desk. 'Are you OK?' she asked, leaning in close. 'You look awful.'

'Thanks,' Jenny said, then she smiled. 'Sorry, Fi, I'm just worried about Carrie.'

'Why? I mean, OK, so she tripped on the rocks but . . .'

'I think she's cross with me,' Jenny confided.

'But why?' Fiona was interested. 'What's happened? Did you have a fight?'

'No . . . but when we were out on Puffin Island I nagged her to keep working. She was tired and she wanted to rest but I begged her not to. I wasn't very nice . . .' Jenny trailed off, ashamed of herself.

'Ah, Carrie wouldn't mind about *that*!' Fiona dismissed Jenny's fears. 'She's not one to bear a grudge. She's always so . . .' she narrowed her eyes, trying to find the right word to describe Carrie, '. . . happy-go-lucky!' she finished.

'That's what I mean,' Jenny whispered. 'Then, if

she isn't upset with me, why hasn't she phoned? I've left loads of messages.'

Fiona was considering this when the bell rang. 'I'll talk to you at break,' she hissed and went to her own desk.

Jenny opened her maths book. Her eyes were swimming with tears and she wiped them away angrily. She was missing Jess, that was it. Coming back to school after having spent so many happy days at home with him was always hard. As she had left for the bus without him this morning, his face had been a picture of despair. Just thinking about it made her sad.

'Can I borrow your ruler?' Penelope James asked her, on the other side. Jenny looked up.

'Sure,' she said. Then, forcing a smile, she decided to put Carrie – and Jess – out of her mind and get on with her maths.

When school finished for the day, Jenny was torn between rushing home to be with Jess and going to visit Carrie. She was troubled by Carrie's silence and badly wanted reassurance.

'Do you want me to come with you?' Fiona asked. She was trying to be kind and Jenny was grateful. For a long time, Fiona had been her enemy and her spiteful tongue had taken away Jenny's confidence.

'Thanks, Fi, but I'll go alone, if you don't mind,' she smiled. 'I'll talk to you tomorrow, OK?'

Fiona nodded as Jenny swung her bulging schoolbag onto her shoulder and hurried off to catch the bus to Cliffbay.

Jenny walked quickly from where the bus dropped her to Cliff House. Mrs Turner's mini was parked in the drive. That was a good sign – they must be at home. She wondered why she felt so nervous. Even if Carrie *had* been offended by her remarks on Puffin Island, she wasn't going to eat her!

Jenny rang the bell. It was opened almost immediately by Mrs Turner. Jenny stared. Carrie's mum didn't look her usual groomed self. Her hair hadn't been brushed and it looked dirty; and the bright lipstick she normally wore was missing, making her face appear pale and tired.

'Hello, Jenny,' she said, sounding subdued.

'Hello,' Jenny stammered in her confusion. 'Um . . . I've come to see Carrie. I wondered if she was sick, because . . .'

'She's not very well, actually, Jenny,' Mrs Turner said. 'In fact, she's resting right now – so I won't disturb her, if you don't mind.'

'No, of course . . . I was worried . . .' Jenny finished.

'Yes, well – don't be!' Mrs Turner snapped. Then her voice softened. 'I'm sorry, love. We'll get in touch with you . . . soon, all right?'

'All right,' Jenny repeated, bewildered. Why wouldn't Mrs Turner let her go up and see Carrie? She stepped back and looked up at Carrie's bedroom window. She almost expected her friend to be peering down at her, her nose flattened against the pane, making a ghastly, comical face. But the lilac curtains in Carrie's window were drawn.

'Bye,' she said, in a small voice, looking back at Mrs Turner. But the door had already been shut. Mrs Turner had gone back inside.

Jenny walked slowly back to the bus stop. Nothing felt right. She was convinced, more than ever, that Carrie just didn't want to see her. She must have decided that Jenny wasn't worth having as a friend and was trying to avoid her.

She struggled not to cry as the bus jolted along the rough road towards the stop near Windy Hill. She trudged her way to the gate and was so wrapped up in her misery that she failed to see Jess streaking across the farmyard towards her – until he was leaping up joyously, his front feet on her chest, licking at her cheeks and making her laugh.

'Jess! Oh, darling Jess! You're my friend, aren't you? My *best* friend! I missed you today, too!'

Inside the big kitchen, Jenny slung her schoolbag on the floor. Mrs Grace was slicing onions, a large brown pot of tea on the table in front of her. 'There's juice in the fridge, Jenny,' she said. 'How was the first day back at school?'

'Carrie wasn't there,' Jenny said, not really answering the question. 'I went to her house after school and her mum said she wasn't very well.'

'There!' Ellen Grace said triumphantly. 'What did I tell you?'

'It still shouldn't stop her from *ringing*,' Jenny said mutinously. 'She's not at death's door!' She poured herself a glass of orange and rummaged in the tin for a biscuit. 'I'm going to take Jess for a walk, now,' she said.

'Any homework?' Mrs Grace asked, raising an eyebrow, being playfully stern.

'Not on the first day back!' Jenny slid out of the door, Jess at her heels.

Jenny headed towards Darktarn Keep, the place she always went to when she wanted to be alone with her thoughts. From up there on the knoll that overlooked Windy Hill, she could see all the way down into Cliffbay, and across the sea to the shadowy outline of Puffin Island.

The late afternoon sun was warm on her back as she walked. Jess ambled along at her side, his tongue lolling happily. But suddenly, the collie stopped, and lifted a paw. He sniffed the air.

'What is it?' Jenny asked him.

The answer arrived in the form of Orla, David's Border collie. She rushed up to greet Jess, her tail wagging. David was ambling along on the path, swinging a stick.

'David!' Jenny called. 'Hello.' She waved. Concerned as she was about Carrie, she was determined to be friendly.

'Hi,' he said, coming over.

'Hello. How did you enjoy your first day at school?'

'Oh, it was OK,' David said, watching Jess playing with Orla. 'I miss my mates, you know . . . from my other school.'

'I looked for you on the bus today. I went down to Cliffbay this afternoon,' Jenny said warmly.

'My dad fetched me,' David said. 'First day and all that.'

'Why did you have to move to Cliffbay?' Jenny asked, as she fell into step beside him.

David's face darkened. He brushed a lock of hair out of his eyes. 'Oh, my father's . . . um . . . it's a business thing, you know.' He changed the subject. 'Look, I was going to go to the SSPCA centre at Graston, that place where they've taken the birds we saved. To see how they're doing. Do you want to come?'

'Oh!' Jenny said, surprised. 'Yes . . . but, do you think it's OK to just drop in? Will they mind?'

'Nah!' said David, grinning. 'We rescued them, didn't we? We've got a right to know if they survived.'

'OK, then,' Jenny smiled. 'Do you know where to go?'

'Yeah, my dad showed me. It's not far,' he answered.

David was quiet as they walked along. Jenny found it difficult to get him to talk much about his life before he came to Cliffbay. Whenever she asked a direct question, David managed to ask a question of his own. She found herself telling him all about Jess's birth.

The SSPCA centre was a small, purpose-built hospital for injured wildlife. There was a reception area with a circle of comfortable chairs and a table with magazines on it. 'It's like the dentist,' David whispered. He had left Orla tied up outside. Jess had come in with Jenny.

At the desk, a young woman was tapping away at a computer keyboard. Her blonde hair was held back in a ponytail and she had a scattering of pale freckles across the bridge of her nose. Jenny guessed she was about twenty years old. She looked up when Jenny approached and took off her reading glasses. 'Can I help you?' she asked pleasantly.

'My name's Jenny Miles,' Jenny began. 'My friend David and I helped to rescue some birds from Puffin Island at the weekend. We wondered how they were.'

The woman got up. 'Would you like to come through and visit our patients?' she smiled. 'You'd be very welcome.'

Jenny grinned in surprise. 'Thank you,' she said, watching as the receptionist came round the desk.

When the woman saw the collie, who was lying down, worrying a burr out of the fur on his paw with his teeth, she bent down to stroke him. 'Hello, gorgeous,' she said. 'You'll have to wait out here, I'm afraid.' Then she looked up at Jenny and David. 'I'm Sarah, by the way. Sarah Taylor.'

Leaving Jess resting comfortably in the waiting-room, Jenny and David followed Sarah through a pair of double doors and down a linoleum-floored corridor. The room she took them to was enormous, made up of a series of pens for the recovering birds. Hanging on the wall, above some shallow tin baths, was a selection of what looked to Jenny like coiled garden hosepipes. The room was very hot.

'Phew!' said David, looking around. 'It looks more like a torture chamber than a hospital.'

Sarah laughed. 'I hope not! Most of the birds you brought in are doing very nicely, thank you! She pointed to the pipes roped up against the wall. Those are high-pressure hoses. We use them for washing the oil off the birds.'

Jenny walked about, peeping in the birds. They were huddled under heat lamps, some with their heads tucked under their wings. There were no traces of oil on their feathers now.

'I heard about your rescue,' Sarah said admiringly. 'Well done. But, there were five of you, weren't there?'

'Yes,' Jenny told her. 'David's dad, and my friends Carrie and Fiona were with us. Only Carrie fell when she was out on the island and she's been sick ever since.'

'Really?' Sarah sounded concerned. 'That's a shame. What's wrong with her?'

'I don't really know,' Jenny confessed. 'She's my best friend but I haven't been able to see her yet. Her mum says she needs rest and shouldn't be disturbed.'

'I can see that must be very worrying for you, not knowing what's going on,' Sarah said gravely. She seemed very understanding and Jenny warmed to her immediately.

'Do you work here all the time?' she asked Sarah.

'Well, I'm a volunteer,' Sarah replied. 'That means I come when I'm needed – and I'm learning as I go along.' She smiled. 'There's a small team of people who come in when a crisis like this one arises. That's why we're always very grateful when people like you and your friends want to help.'

'Oh, we'd love to help – any time,' Jenny offered. 'I'm sure Carrie and Fiona would love to come along too.'

'Well, I'll tell you what, why don't you all come in when Carrie's better? It would be nice to meet her. And your other friend too, of course.' Sarah smiled.

'Thanks,' Jenny said, surprised again. She had imagined that she and David would be allowed just a glimpse of the birds, before being hurried out of the centre. Sarah was making them feel very welcome.

The young woman glanced at her watch. 'It's almost time for the night-time assistant to come in for the next shift,' Sarah said. 'So, I'm off home in a moment. Come back again when you can, all right?'

'Yes,' Jenny said, smiling. 'Thanks, we will.' She would tell Carrie about Sarah and the centre. Tomorrow at school, when Carrie was back. Carrie would love it here and it would be sure to cheer her up. Jenny could hardly wait for the next day.

6

When Carrie didn't appear at school the following day, Jenny began to feel a sense of dread. Her lessons passed in a blur. She couldn't find a grain of enthusiasm for anything.

'She must be really sick,' Fiona said gloomily, at breaktime. 'Too sick even to come to the phone.'

'Oh, don't,' Jenny begged. 'I can't bear to think about it.'

'I know!' Fiona said, suddenly sounding cheerful. 'Why don't we buy some chocolates – her favourites

– and take them round to the house?'

Jenny smiled wanly. 'No, Fi, we'd better not,' she said. 'Mrs Turner said *they* would get in touch with *us*. We shouldn't interfere.'

At home that afternoon, Jenny confided in Jess. She sat on the floor in her bedroom, with the collie curled against her, resting his head in her lap. 'It's hard for me to believe that Carrie's too ill to speak on the phone,' Jenny told him, flattening his ears and watching them spring back. 'If I were sick, I'd ring her. I mean, she must know how worried I am.'

Jess looked at Jenny, his head cocked to one side, his soft brown eyes full of understanding.

'I'm so glad I've got you!' Jenny said, kissing the top of his soft white nose. Without Carrie around, Jenny was feeling particularly alone. Her nineteen-year-old brother, Matt, hadn't made it back to Windy Hill for two weekends in a row now. He was away in England on a field trip and Jenny didn't know when she would next see him.

Mrs Grace was there, of course, and she had listened patiently to Jenny going on about Carrie for three days now. Her father, who had noticed Jenny's glum face, had dismissed her fears with a confident chuckle. 'The sort of friendship you have with Carrie Turner is not going to dissolve overnight because of a few harsh words spoken under pressure, lass,' he said. 'I promise you that.'

Jenny didn't know what to think any more. 'Maybe I should write to her,' she said to Jess, who, alerted by the brighter tone in her voice, stood up and looked around the room expectantly. It made Jenny giggle. 'Silly boy,' she said. 'Oh, well, that's enough brooding. A letter is too formal, anyway. Let's go and see what's for supper.'

Jess barked his approval.

The geography lesson had started when Carrie appeared in the classroom the next day. Jenny looked up, overjoyed, as Carrie came across to her desk.

'Sorry I'm late,' she said to the teacher, who nodded and smiled. Carrie slipped in behind her desk and propped her chin in her hands. She didn't even glance across at Jenny but looked straight at the blackboard, where Mrs Johnson was drawing a map.

Jenny felt an ache deep in her chest. That proved it! Carrie must be cross with her.

She tore a piece of paper from her notebook and scribbled: *Welcome back. I missed you*, on it. She slipped it onto her friend's desk. Carrie was smiling at David, now sitting at the desk to her left. Jenny's ache worsened.

Then Carrie looked over and smiled. 'Thanks,' she whispered, waving the tiny note. Almost as quickly, she turned her attention back to the blackboard.

Jenny was relieved and puzzled all at once. Carrie seemed . . . somehow . . . different. It was as though someone had blown out the spark that made Carrie who she was. This was a quieter Carrie, a Carrie held in check by some mysterious, invisible force. Even her eyes seemed to have lost their strong, sparkly blue colour, and faded to a wishy-washy pastel. What *was* going on?

When the bell went at mid-morning break, Jenny went straight to the part of the school grounds where she, Carrie, and sometimes Fiona, usually met. She sank onto the grass and waited. Each minute seemed to tick by like an hour.

'Where's Carrie?' Fiona asked, joining her.

'I don't know,' Jenny said carefully. 'She had her art lesson, but I thought she would meet us here at break.'

'Well, then, if she's coming to meet you she can't be cross with you, after all?' Fiona said.

'No,' Jenny agreed, not feeling at all sure of this. 'She didn't seem it.'

'Here she comes now,' Fiona said. 'Hi, Carrie!'

Jenny felt a hot flush creep into her face. She wanted to talk to Carrie alone. Now Fiona was here, she wouldn't get the chance.

Carrie, who usually came belting up the field singing the latest pop song, was walking slowly towards them. 'Hello,' she called, smiling.

'Are you better?' Fiona rushed in. 'Have you seen the new history teacher? He's Italian!'

'I've been worried about you,' Jenny said softly, annoyed with Fiona for prattling on. 'What was the matter?'

'Ugh! Some bug,' said Carrie, dismissively. 'Have I missed loads of work?'

'Yeah, loads,' said Fiona unhelpfully. 'Did you throw up?'

'Fiona!' Jenny said. She suddenly felt protective of Carrie. It was normally Carrie who kept an eye on Jenny. She realised she was peering closely at her friend, looking for signs that Carrie wasn't annoyed with her. All she could see was a calm, ashen face. There were no clues at all.

'Yes, I did, if you must know,' Carrie was saying to Fiona.

'Carrie . . .' Jenny began, but her sentence was interrupted by the bell. Break was over already. 'Meet

75

here at lunch-break?' she asked hopefully.

'Um . . . no,' Carrie was vague. 'I'll be going home at lunch-time today. My mum's coming to fetch me.'

'Oh!' Jenny was stung. There would be no opportunity to talk to her friend at lunch-time. Jenny didn't know how much longer she could bear it. She looked at Carrie. Her pale, weary face showed no emotion but her eyes challenged Jenny. *Don't make a fuss*, they seemed to plead. *Don't say anything. Leave me alone.*

Carrie must have seen the hurt in Jenny's face. 'Can I borrow your books? To catch up on notes?' she asked.

Jenny was relieved. 'Yes, of course,' she said.

'Thanks,' Carrie said, and began to walk away. Jenny looked at Fiona helplessly.

'Well!' Fiona said, after Carrie had gone. 'She wasn't exactly friendly, was she? Maybe you're right, after all.'

Jenny nodded, preoccupied with her own thoughts. She realised she hadn't told Carrie about the SSPCA centre, and meeting Sarah. There was so much Jenny wanted to say. She was longing to have a chance to talk – really talk – to her friend.

Jess was especially affectionate when Jenny got home.

He wouldn't leave her side, sitting beside her when she sat, putting his nose gently into her hand or his paw into her lap. 'I'm OK, boy, really I am,' Jenny reassured him. But the collie seemed to sense the depths of Jenny's sadness and his eyes were dull.

'Why don't you go over and try talking to Carrie?' Mrs Grace suggested.

Jenny felt a stab of guilt. Poor Mrs Grace had been so kind. Jenny was certain she was sick of looking at her miserable, moping face. But she couldn't help herself. 'I've tried that, remember?' she said. 'Mrs Turner turned me away.' She was interrupted by a voice from the door.

'Hello, love.' Fraser Miles had taken off a wellington boot and was hopping around on one sock. 'You look as though you've just lost your best friend,' he joked.

'Dad!' cried Jenny, wounded by the remark.

Fraser Miles's face flooded with guilt. 'Oh, Jen!' he said, mortified, and pulled off the other boot. He padded over to her. 'Forgive me, lass. I was only joking – don't tell me this thing with Carrie is still going on?'

Jenny nodded, her eyes filling with tears.

'Something's up,' Mrs Grace told him, slipping a comforting arm round Jenny's sagging shoulders.

'And it's clear Carrie won't share whatever's troubling her with Jenny.'

'Would you like me to try and talk to Mrs Turner?' Fraser asked.

'No!' Jenny said quickly. 'Thanks, but that would make me look desperate. I have got other friends . . . I suppose,' she trailed off. It was unthinkable, losing Carrie as a friend.

'Go over there!' Mr Miles urged. 'Go and hammer on the door and ask what's going on. Haven't you got an excuse for a visit?'

Jenny's face brightened. She suddenly remembered the school work. Jess, looking at her and pricked up his ears. 'Yes, that's it. I promised her she could have a look at my school books – the work she missed when she was away. That's the perfect reason to go round. After all, she did ask for my help,' she said.

'Well, then . . .' said Fraser, relieved to see Jenny more determined. 'I think this calls for a cup of good, strong tea, Ellen!'

'I'll put the kettle on,' Mrs Grace said, smiling.

It began to rain just as Jenny left the house to visit Carrie. It was grey and showery, which suited Jenny's mood. Jess walked solemnly beside her, his tail out straight. He seemed reluctant to bound ahead in his usual fashion, preferring to keep pace with Jenny.

The sky was the colour of an old bruise by the time she reached Cliff House. Rain was pelting at her from every angle and she ran, trying to dodge it, until she arrived in a rush at the front door. She was soaked, but pleased about it. Surely Carrie's mum couldn't turn her away in this weather.

'Oh, Jenny,' said Mrs Turner, matter-of-factly, opening the door. 'It's you.' She peered out, as though she had only just noticed the change in the weather. 'Gosh, just look at that rain! You'd better come in. And Jess too . . . come through into the kitchen.'

Jenny stepped into the hall and slipped off her shoes. She wiped her wet face with the flat of her hands. 'I've brought these books for Carrie,' she said, taking a plastic bag from inside her coat and following Mrs Turner.

The kitchen was brightly lit. Jenny loved the colours in the room. Carrie's mum was an artist and had brought the walls to life with warm, bright shades of deep yellow and strong green. It had always seemed a happy room to Jenny.

'Here, Jess,' said Mrs Turner. The collie trotted over and sat down while she rubbed him all over with an old towel. 'What a puddly day,' she said, and sighed.

'How's Carrie?' Jenny asked, looking down at her feet.

'She's in her bedroom,' Mrs Turner said, avoiding the question. 'I'll go up and see if she wants a bit of company, shall I?'

Jenny and Jess were alone in the kitchen. Jess lay down and put his nose on his paws. He gave a big sigh. 'It's all right, Jess,' Jenny whispered. 'There's bound to be an explanation for all this, you'll see.' She put a comforting hand on his head and looked around her.

There was a bunch of lavender in a little glass vase on the table in front of her. Under it was a letter. It was lying open, and the words 'Dr Ian David' caught Jenny's eye. Rather guiltily, she leaned forward to read it, looking first at the letter heading across the top of the page. It was from Greybridge Hospital.

Jenny scanned the typed letter quickly, knowing she had no right to do so. The brief words confirmed an appointment for Carrie to attend a clinic during the following week. That was all. Jenny felt her heart tighten in her chest. Hospital! Then Carrie was more sick than she was letting on. Jenny quickly replaced the vase and sat back in her chair. She felt herself tremble slightly. She heard Mrs Turner coming down the stairs.

'You can go up and see her, if you like,' Carrie's mum said, from the door. 'Leave Jess here with me. I'll bring up some drinks. Coke?'

'Yes, please. Thank you,' Jenny said, in confusion, picking up the carrier bag. Now that she was at last going to confront her friend, she felt tongue-tied with nerves.

'Jenny?' Mrs Turner said softly, as Jenny headed for the stairs. 'Don't stay too long, will you?'

Jenny stared at her. Then she remembered her manners. 'No, of course not, Mrs Turner,' she said. 'I won't stay long.'

The door to Carrie's room was closed. Jenny knocked lightly.

'Hi,' Carrie called, from the other side.

Jenny eased the door open and peered around it. 'Hello,' she said, as cheerfully as she could. 'I've brought you the books you wanted.'

Carrie was lying on her bed. She was propped up against several pillows, her feet crossed at the ankles. Her hair was loose, spreading around her in a cloud of red and making her face look a ghostly white by contrast. She was holding a comic in her hand.

'You shouldn't have bothered to come over in this rain,' Carrie said vacantly. 'It could have waited.'

Jenny sat on the chair in the room and looked at her friend. She couldn't think of what to say. In the awkward silence, Jenny thought she was going to cry. *Just say what you've come to say, Jenny*, she told herself. But her courage failed her.

'How are you . . . feeling?' she eventually asked Carrie.

'Fine,' Carrie replied, too quickly.

'Really?' Jenny pressed her.

'Oh, for heaven's sake!' Carrie said irritably. 'Stop looking at me like that.'

Tears stung Jenny's eyes and spilled down her cheeks. She couldn't hold them back any longer. A

great sob escaped from her. It sounded awful in the quiet of the room. She covered her face with her hands, hot with emotion.

Carrie said nothing. She didn't move.

'Carrie,' Jenny mumbled, through her tears. 'Please tell me . . . talk to me. Tell me what's wrong. What *is* it?'

7

Carrie swung her legs off the bed and sat facing Jenny. She pushed her springy hair behind her ears and gave a huge sigh. 'Oh, Jen,' she said, mournfully. 'I'm sorry for shutting you out.'

'Really?' Jenny asked hopefully. 'You've been so . . . different . . . at first I thought I'd upset you . . .'

'No, it's not that. It's just that I'm *angry* – at the whole world!' Carrie shouted, making her hands into fists and punching wildly at her pillow. Jenny was startled.

'But what's happened?' she said again. 'Please, you must tell me.'

'Well, OK,' Carrie said. 'But promise not to tell another living soul, right?'

'Right,' said Jenny. Her mind was racing, wondering what terrible thing Carrie was going to tell her. Surely, whatever illness she had, she could be made well again?

'Before I came to live here I was very ill,' Carrie said. 'Then I got better – but now the sickness has come back.'

'What kind of sickness?' Jenny wrinkled her nose and frowned.

'Leukaemia. Acute lymphoblastic leukaemia, to be precise. Cancer of the blood. It makes you feel rotten,' Carrie finished. She lay back on her bed and gazed up at a photograph of a basket of tiny kittens, pinned on the wall.

'But can't the doctors do something?' Jenny asked, thinking of the letter she'd seen on the kitchen table.

'They're trying,' Carrie told her. 'It isn't an easy thing to cure.'

'But you'll have to go into hospital?'

'Maybe,' Carrie said. 'You see, the cancer attacks the white blood cells, which are called lymphocytes, inside the marrow of your bones. I may have to have some new marrow to replace the sick marrow – that is, if they can find some for me.'

Jenny frowned at her friend. She was obviously very knowledgeable about this confusing illness. 'Why didn't you tell me you'd had it before?' she asked.

'I was trying to forget about it,' Carrie told her. 'I thought it was all behind me and I'd never have to think about it again. It was a horrible time,' she added.

'How did you catch it?' Jenny said.

Carrie smiled. 'You don't *catch* cancer!' she said. 'You just get it.'

'But how does it make you feel?' Jenny voice had a tremor in it.

'Tired – because I've got so many white blood cells being made in my bone marrow,' Carrie explained. 'It's bad to have too many of them, you see. They break down the marrow in your bones and seep out into your blood.'

Jenny chewed at a fingernail. There were so many questions going round in her head. She felt bewildered and afraid. 'You're going to get better . . . soon, though, aren't you?' she asked Carrie.

'Who knows?' Carrie shrugged and looked up at the ceiling.

'Who *knows*?' Jenny repeated, blinking. 'You mean, you may *not* get better?' The terrible truth of what she was hearing was beginning to sink in. Carrie didn't answer her.

'I don't want anyone to know, OK? Not even Fiona,' she said firmly.

'But . . . why not?' Jenny asked, faintly.

'I don't want people feeling sorry for me, that's why,' Carrie told her. She sat up again, frowning fiercely.

In a trice, Jenny was out of her chair. She threw her arms round Carrie and hugged her tight. 'You *are* going to get better!' she said. 'Of course you are. Think of all the wonderful medicines there are in the world today.' She spoke into Carrie's ear, their cheeks pressed together.

Carrie hugged her back. 'I'm scared, Jen,' she whispered.

'Carrie,' said Jenny, facing her. 'There are so many people who love you and want to help. We'll all help you! And I'm sure you're going to get better.'

Jenny didn't feel as confident as she sounded. Her words seemed hollow in her ears and inside, her tummy was churning with fear. What if Carrie didn't get better? Jenny realised, with a little shock, that she was going to have to be the strong one of the two of them, from now on. No more leaning on bright, devil-may-care, Carrie. Carrie would need Jenny's strength and support. She was going to have to be the positive one in the friendship to see her through.

'So many people love you,' she said again, '. . . and, look, here's one of them now!'

The door to Carrie's bedroom had been nosed open. Jess's head appeared in the crack. He peeped through hesitantly.

'Jess!' said Carrie, laughing. 'Hello, boy!' Jess bounded into the room, his tail wagging furiously. He pranced about, delighted to have discovered Jenny.

'Has Jess found his way up there to you?' called Mrs Turner from the stairs. She came into the room. 'I went outside to hang some washing on the line and he was out of the kitchen and upstairs in a moment.'

'It's nice to see him,' Carrie said, hugging the collie. She smiled at her mother as Jess licked her hand.

'Here are your drinks.' Mrs Turner put two glasses of Coke on the bookshelf. She turned and looked anxiously at Carrie and her face brightened. 'You look more cheerful!' she smiled at her daughter. 'I'm glad you came, Jenny.'

Jenny squeezed Carrie's hand. 'So am I,' she said.

★ ★ ★

Jenny remembered to tell her friend about the SSPCA centre and what Sarah Taylor had said, and then she left Carrie to rest.

Walking up the lane through Graston towards Windy Hill later, Jenny gave in to her tears. She had been cheerful when she had said goodbye to Carrie but now there was no one about to see or hear her crying.

The first lights of early evening were coming on in the houses dotted about the hillside. Storm clouds were still glowering in a low, dark sky, though the rain had gone. Her shoulders shook as she walked and her throat ached from her sobbing. Jess, his tail drooping, slunk along at her side. From time to time, he pushed his cold, wet nose into the palm of her hand. 'I'm all right, Jess,' she stuttered. 'I'm just sad about Carrie.' The Border collie whined and hung his head.

Jenny wiped her eyes on her sleeve as she went through the gates of the farm. Ahead of her she saw her father, carrying a bale of straw into the big barn. She followed him in. It was gloomy inside and she was glad of it. She didn't want him to see her red, tear-stained face. 'Hi, Dad,' she said in a small voice.

Fraser Miles looked round. 'Jenny, love!' he said.

'How did your visit to Carrie go?'

Nell, Jess's mother, was sniffing her puppy all over, curiously identifying the strange places he'd visited. Jess's tail thumped in greeting, then he hurried over and lay quietly at Jenny's side. She had slumped onto a nearby bale.

'Ah . . . didn't go well?' Fraser Miles frowned. He titled Jenny's chin with his finger and looked into her troubled face.

Jenny crumpled. 'Oh, Dad,' she wept, 'Carrie wasn't cross with me. It's just that she's ill – she's got . . . leukaemia!' She blurted out the news that Carrie had made her promise to keep to herself.

'What?' Mr Miles was startled.

Jenny nodded miserably 'Will she get better?' she pleaded, knowing that her father couldn't know the answer to this.

He sat down beside Jenny and put an arm around her. He had gone quite pale. 'There's always a chance, lass,' he said softly. 'But it might mean a long, brave fight.'

'She asked me not to tell you, or anybody, but there are so many questions I want answered. I didn't want to ask her too many,' Jenny said.

'Well, there are things that can be done,' Fraser Miles said. 'For a start, there is a type of treatment called chemotherapy. That's using special drugs that fight the abnormal cells growing in the body. That's what cancer is.'

'Carrie said something about getting some new bone marrow?' Jenny said.

'A transplant, yes,' Mr Miles nodded. 'I don't know a lot about it but I know that the doctors have to find someone whose bone marrow will be exactly the same as Carrie's. Then they take it out of the healthy person and put it into her.'

'But if nobody *knows* Carrie's sick, how will they be able to offer her their bone marrow?' Jenny wailed. 'I mean, could I give her some of mine?'

'Well, that's a noble thought,' Jenny's dad squeezed her shoulder. 'And a brave one, too. But I expect the right match of marrow is likely to come from people in Carrie's immediate family.'

'You won't tell anyone?' Jenny asked him. 'I promised her . . .'

'No, it will be our secret. And if you need to talk to someone other than Carrie about it, you'll come to me, won't you?' Mr Miles hugged her.

'I'm sorry that I'm not being more help to you on the farm,' Jenny said.

'I don't expect it, lass. You've got your own problems, just now,' her father replied.

Jess whimpered, looking up at Jenny with liquid brown eyes. She put out a hand to him. 'I've got you,' she said to her father, 'and I've got Jess. I'm a very lucky girl.'

Jenny was preoccupied during supper and hardly said a word. If Ellen Grace noticed, she didn't comment. 'I've made up a marvellous dish of leftover bits and pieces for Jess,' she told Jenny, brightly. 'Had a good old clear-out of the fridge. He'll have a feast tomorrow.'

Jenny smiled her thanks. 'I'm tired,' she said. 'I think I'll go to bed.'

'I'll let Jess out last thing, shall I?' Fraser Miles asked. He blew her a kiss. 'Sleep tight,' he said and winked. Jenny was glad she'd confided in her father. The news about Carrie was too much for her to bear all alone.

She walked slowly up the stairs to her bedroom. Her bedside lamp, with its creamy yellow shade, gave the room a lovely, lemony warmth. Jenny had chosen to have the walls painted yellow again when Windy Hill had been restored after the fire, and she was glad. It was a cosy, cheerful colour. A photograph of her beautiful mother stood in a frame on her desk, replacing the one she'd had of her as a young girl that had been charred to cinders. How she wished it were possible to tell her mother about Carrie, and to ask her what to do.

There was a faint scraping at the door. When Jenny opened it she found Jess was sitting outside, looking up at her lovingly, his tail swishing gently against the carpet on the landing. 'Oh, Jess,' Jenny smiled, her heart melting. 'Do Mrs Grace and Dad know you've come up here?'

The collie slipped quickly into the room and lay down on Jenny's carpet. His coat smelled of heather, and rain, and there was mud on all four of his white feet.

She sat on the floor beside him, and put an arm round his neck. 'I'm glad you're here,' she told him, smoothing his ears. Jess rolled over onto his back, all four feet in the air, so Jenny could tickle his tummy.

'You know, I'm going to be the best friend to Carrie *ever*,' Jenny said. 'I'm going to show her that she needn't be scared all on her own. Mum always said that sharing a problem halves it. You can help too, Jess. We've got to make her see that she doesn't have to hide away – and we've got to find somebody with healthy marrow in their bones to give to her.' Lying upside down, Jess blinked his caramel-brown eyes at her knowingly.

Jenny was suddenly more tired than she'd ever felt before. Her eyelids began to close. She slid down onto the carpet, curling up next to Jess, and closed her eyes. The warmth of the dog and his soft fur was comforting. She could feel Jess breathing.

'I don't know what I'd do without you,' she murmured, and fell asleep.

8

Sunlight slanted in through the gap in Jenny's curtains and woke her. She heard the crunch of boots on gravel in the farmyard below her window. Curled up in her duvet, she recognised her father's long, low whistle, as he put Jake and Nell through their paces, shepherding the young sheep to the field for grazing. These were familiar and comforting sounds, and they filled Jenny with a sense of security.

Then she became aware of another sound. A gentle snuffling, muddled with a more strenuous snore. She sat up, surprised, and looked to the floor. Jess was stretched out on his side, sleeping deeply. His back legs twitched and his nose quivered. He gave a grunt, then sighed.

'Jess!' whispered Jenny. 'How on earth did you manage to stay in here all night long? If Dad finds out . . .' Jess lifted his head. He blinked dopey eyes at her, then sat up and yawned. Stretching luxuriously, he reached out with a wet tongue to lick Jenny's cheek. She giggled. 'Good morning to you, too, sleepyhead.'

'Jenny?' There was a gentle tapping at the door.

'Ooh, quick!' Jenny said to Jess. 'Here's Mrs Grace . . .' The door opened.

Mrs Grace stepped into the room as Jess was trying to disappear under Jenny's bed. Only his tail stuck out. 'I can see you,' she said, trying not to smile. She turned to Jenny, 'Your father discovered you both asleep up here last night and decided to leave Jess with you. I can't think why . . . but don't think you're going to make a habit of it.' She chuckled.

'Oh, we won't, Mrs Grace,' Jenny grinned. 'Will we, Jess?' Jess popped his head out from under the bed. They could hear his tail thumping on the floor under the mattress.

'Up you get, love,' Ellen Grace said, opening Jenny's

curtains. 'You've had a little lie in – and you're going to be late for school if you don't hurry.'

Jess ran to the door and looked back at Jenny, his tail going from side to side. She laughed. 'Jess wants that feast you promised him last night,' she said, jumping out of bed.

Mrs Grace nodded. 'Don't be long,' she called, as she left the room.

Jenny ran lightly across the landing to the bathroom. Then, she remembered Carrie and her heart squeezed tight in her chest. 'Carrie!' she whispered, to herself. Carrie, too, would be waking up now – but to another day of feeling unwell, and frightened, and having to hide it. Jenny grabbed her toothbrush. Her friend needed her. There was not a minute to waste.

On the way to the hall for assembly, Jenny managed to get Carrie alone. 'At breaktime,' she said, 'will you meet me somewhere other than our usual place?'

'What for?' said Carrie, glumly.

Jenny couldn't get over the change in her friend. Her energy and enthusiasm had drained away. The vitality and curiosity she had so envied in Carrie had gone.

'Just meet me, will you?' Jenny smiled. 'Outside the history room, OK?'

Carrie nodded, and looked down at her feet. Jenny felt a surge of triumph. At least she wouldn't have to worry about Fiona, and possibly David, tagging along, and would be able to talk to Carrie openly.

Carrie was waiting when Jenny arrived at their meeting place at lunch-time. She was picking at a packet of crisps. 'I'm never even hungry any more,' she announced, as Jenny came over and sat down. Carrie held out the crisps. 'D'you want these?'

'Thanks,' Jenny took them. She noticed that Carrie's eyes were wet. 'Are you OK?' she asked.

Carrie shook her head. 'We've had some bad news,' she said. 'Some friends of my mum and dad have been tested to see if the marrow in their bones matched mine . . .'

'And . . .?' Jenny was staring at Carrie, her hopes were high.

'They don't,' she said. 'Marrow has to be genetically compatible . . .'

'What?' Jenny said. 'What's that?'

'Matched exactly to my own marrow, to fit in with mine, you know. But it doesn't.' Carrie sighed. 'Neither Mr nor Mrs Bailey's.'

'Could I have a go?' Jenny said, her eyes shining. 'You know I *would* . . . what do you have to do?'

'You have to have your blood tested, first. Then, if the tests show that it's any good to me, you go into hospital for a bit. They stick a needle into your hip and pull out some marrow, then test it. It's called aspiration,' Carrie explained.

Jenny winced. 'Ouch,' she said, then regretted it. 'Oh, but I'd do it, Carrie,' she added quickly, loyally. 'If it would help you to get better.'

'You get these neat little puncture marks in your skin, just like a vampire bat has feasted on you,' Carrie said, showing a spark of her old sense of humour.

Jenny laughed.

'But there's got to be a perfect match of cell tissue,' Carrie went on, 'or my body will reject it.' It sounded complicated to Jenny.

'Isn't there anybody else you could ask to give you some of their marrow?' she asked. 'Some of the other people in your family, maybe?'

'Tried them all,' Carrie stated. 'The last time I was sick, we tried them. There is something called a register of donors – a place where anyone can just go in and give their blood and marrow for testing. Then it's kept in a kind of bank for sick people who might need it.'

'And?' Jenny urged. 'Have you been to this bank?'

'Yes,' Carrie sighed. 'There is nothing in there that's a match for me.'

'But there must be!' Jenny cried.

Carrie shook her head. 'Everyone has to die,' she reasoned, though her lower lip was wobbling. 'I'll just die a little sooner, that's all.'

'You're not going to die!' Jenny said. 'You're not! That's why you've got to tell everyone about your sickness, Carrie. The more people that know about it, the more people there will be to help you.'

'I suppose you're right,' Carrie said quietly. 'I've definitely felt better since I told you about it.'

Jenny smiled. 'And it'll get difficult to pretend, won't it?' she asked. 'People would wonder about you, and whisper and things. It's best to tell them.'

'I will have to go into hospital soon to have my next drug treatment, anyway. So I won't be at school for days at a time. Also, my hair will probably fall out. It did last time,' Carrie said.

Jenny tried to imagine Carrie without her lovely mop of coppery red hair and began to cry.

Carrie put an arm round her. 'Don't cry, Jen,' she said.

'It's OK. We're going to find someone to give you their bone marrow,' Jenny said through her tears, with as much determination as she could. 'We *are*.'

'Yes,' said Carrie, smiling. 'Yes, you're right. There might be a chance. You'll help me, won't you?

As the bell went for the end of break Jenny hugged her, reluctant to let her go.

Jenny told Mrs Grace about Carrie's sickness. Remembering the way Carrie had tried not to give in to her tears when she had spoken about dying made Jenny cry all over again.

'Oh, Jenny, love,' Mrs Grace said sadly, putting her arms round Jenny and holding her tight. 'It's always a very frightening thing when someone we love is so ill. You feel hopeless, don't you?'

'That's it,' sobbed Jenny, burying her face in Mrs Grace's shoulder, 'that's exactly how I feel. All sort of hopeless inside. I want to do something to help, but I don't know what.'

'Well, it sounds to me as though you're doing just what Carrie would want. You're being positive and showing her you care. That's a good start,' she said. Mrs Grace smoothed Jenny's hair.

It felt lovely and made her a bit calmer, as though she didn't have any more tears to cry. It wasn't the same as it might have been talking to her mother, but Ellen Grace was kind and Jenny was beginning to feel the housekeeper really cared about her. She realised that working at Windy Hill wasn't *just* a job for Mrs Grace any more. It was her father, herself, and Matt and Jess, that mattered to her. Shyly, Jenny wound her arms round Mrs Grace's neck. She kissed her lightly on her rosy, scented cheek. 'Thank you,' she said. 'Thanks for being here.'

Then Jenny pulled away and took the handkerchief Mrs Grace offered her. She blew her nose. There was a slight noise and she looked up at the door to see her father standing there. He was smiling.

On Friday Carrie was absent from school again. Jenny knew that she had gone into hospital for her chemotherapy. She had even given Jenny permission to ask the teacher to announce to the class that she had leukaemia and to explain what the sickness was.

'There is every chance that Carrie will get well,' said Jenny's form teacher, 'but I want to ask you all for your understanding. I expect you to be gentle and kind and not make Carrie feel awkward or alone. She will need the support of all of us.'

'Can we catch it from her?' Fiona asked Jenny later, miserably.

'You don't *catch* cancer, silly,' Jenny retorted, remembering Carrie's words. 'You just get it.'

'Carrie hasn't even been to see the birds down at the centre yet,' David remembered gloomily.

'Neither have I!' Fiona said. 'I'd like to go.'

'Then we'll go, shall we?' Jenny said, trying to be cheerful and strong for Carrie's other friends. 'Let's go today after school and see how they're getting on.'

'Oh, OK. Meet you on the cliff path at, say, four o'clock?' David agreed. He forced a smile.

'Yes,' Fiona nodded. 'I'll be there, too.'

Jenny decided to leave Jess at Windy Hill. A bird hospital was no place for a collie, even though Sarah Taylor had welcomed him warmly the last time he'd been there. Jenny knew that Jess would behave perfectly, as always, but she didn't want any of the birds to be frightened.

She changed into jeans and a sweatshirt, ran a brush through her honey-brown hair and took the stairs two at a time. Down in the kitchen, Mrs Grace was grating cheese onto a plate. She looked up. 'Are you off somewhere, Jenny?'

'Down to that bird centre place, with David Fergusson and Fiona. I thought I'd leave Jess behind, but I want to spend a little time with him first,' she said. Jess, who was lying just beneath the table on which Mrs Grace was now slicing through a loaf of chunky wholemeal bread, looked up as she spoke and put his head to one side.

'Sorry, Jess,' Jenny stroked him. 'But you'd only have to stay in the waiting-room, like last time.'

'Have a sandwich before you go?' Mrs Grace suggested. 'I'm making a heap of them for your father.'

'Where is he?' Jenny asked, taking one from the plate and biting into it. 'Hmmm, yum,' she mumbled, her mouth full.

'Up in the top field,' Mrs Grace told her. 'Several of the ewes are close to having their lambs now.'

'The first spring lambs!' Jenny breathed. 'Oh, and I've been so wrapped up with Carrie I've hardly spent any time out in the fields.'

'Well, we've had fine weather,' Mrs Grace said, pleased. 'It should be a good lambing this season.' Ellen Grace had grown up in the region and so she knew that the harsh Borders climate could be tough on newly-born lambs.

Jenny whistled and Jess's head shot up. 'Come on, boy,' she said, swallowing the last mouthful of her sandwich. 'Race you to the top field.'

★　★　★

THE DISCOVERY

Jenny found her father examining a heavily pregnant ewe.

'You win, Jess!' she yelled, as she reached the fence to the field moments after the collie. She was out of breath and her tummy ached, and even Jess's sides were heaving as he panted. Mr Miles waved and Jenny climbed over the stile to join him. Jess squeezed under the wire and kept to her heel.

'It's nice to see you up here, lass,' smiled Jenny's dad. He let go of the sheep, and it ambled off, bleating, to the rest of the flock.

'I came to say I'm sorry for not showing more interest in the lambing. It isn't that I don't care about the farm any more. It's just that I've been so busy thinking about Carrie,' Jenny said.

'I know that, love,' Fraser Miles smiled. 'Being a good friend to someone who needs you is more important than being a good farmer's daughter.' He sat down on the slope, his big wellington boots stretched out before him and crossed at the ankles. He patted the grassy mound beside him.

Jenny joined him, leaning against his woolly jumper and sighing. 'Our teacher told the class about Carrie today,' she said, plucking the flecks of straw from his sleeve. 'Don't you think it's better now that everybody knows?'

'Aye, I do,' her father agreed, 'Far better than living with a secret.'

'A terrible secret,' Jenny said in a small voice.

Fraser Miles slipped an arm round her. 'It's not been an easy time, Jen love,' he said quietly. 'Mum . . . going . . . then the fire, and that unfortunate business with Marion . . .'

'Don't remind me!' Jenny shuddered. She hated to think of the horrible time when Marion Stewart had tired to poison Jess. The estate agent was a friend of Fraser Miles and she had come to stay at Windy Hill while Mrs Grace had been in Canada. Marion hadn't like Jess, who had shown an unusual hostility towards her. She had wanted him out of the way – and had almost succeeded. But ultimately, Jess had revealed to everyone Marion's true colours. Jenny reached out for Jess, and pulled him closer. She could not imagine a life without her beloved dog.

'I'd better go,' she said, jumping up. 'I'm meeting David and Fiona and we're going down to the SSPCA center. Can I leave Jess here with you?'

'Of course you can,' grinned Mr Miles. 'He can learn a few more lessons from his mother and father. See you at suppertime, love?'

'Yep,' said Jenny. 'Now, stay there, Jess. Good boy.'

The collie's face fell. His ears went down and he put his chin on his paws.

'She's coming back!' Jenny heard her father laugh, as she went off down the hill.

Even though it had been several days since the tanker's accident, oiled birds were still being found along the coast, and brought in to the SSPCA centre by concerned volunteers. The holding pens were full of recovering birds, huddling together, shivering, under the heat lamps.

Jenny, David and Fiona were taken through to the room with all the hosepipes, where they found Sarah Taylor washing a furious-looking puffin.

Sarah hardly glanced up as she greeted them. 'He's not enjoying this one bit, poor mite,' she said sympathetically.

Fiona covered her eyes as the high-pressure shower blasted against the bird's chest, parting the feathers to the pink skin beneath.

'Isn't that water too hot?' David asked, amazed at the steam coming off the bird. 'Won't it burn it?'

'No,' Sarah assured him. 'The water needs to be really hot, as hot as the bird can bear, to loosen and soften the oil. That's the only way we can get it off.'

'What about using soap?' Jenny asked, feeling

desperately sorry for the poor puffin.

'We do use soap,' Sarah said. 'We wash as much oil as we can off first, then use a special detergent, like washing-up liquid. Then the bird is rinsed again, in soft water, to make certain that all the soap is out of its plumage.'

'How long does it take for them to recover?' Fiona asked, peeking at the struggling bird through a gap in her fingers.

'Usually about a week or two,' Sarah said. She was massaging the liquid soap into the feathers of a small, outstretched wing. The puffin kept turning its head, trying to grab her glove with its beak. 'But, sadly, some don't make it.'

'Oh, that's such a shame,' Jenny said.

'Well, we do our very best to save them,' Sarah told her. 'We feed them a gourmet diet – sand eels and best quality sprats – to build them up. They have a swimming pool too, to make them feel at home.'

'Then, when they are fat and healthy again, what then?' David wanted to know.

'The SSPCA has the job of returning them to the sea,' Sarah smiled. 'Actually, some of the birds you brought in are just about ready to go back. Ah . . . here's Debbie, coming to help me to get this little fellow dry and warm again. There!' Sarah handed the dripping puffin to an assistant, who had come over with a towel. Sarah knelt and began to hose out the porcelain basin, washing the traces of oil and feathers away down the plughole.

'Does anyone want to give me a hand over here?' someone called.

'That's Kim,' Sarah explained. 'She's taking some birds out to the pool. Do you want to help her?'

'Yes please!' David said and hurried over.

'I do, too, please,' Fiona followed David. Before Jenny could move, Sarah spoke.

'How's your friend? Carrie, is it?' she asked.

'Not too good,' Jenny said. She squatted down beside Sarah. 'I've found out what was wrong with her. She's got leukaemia.'

Sarah drew in her breath sharply. She stopped what she was doing and gave Jenny her full attention. 'What shocking news. Poor girl,' she said softly.

'She doesn't mind my telling,' Jenny added. 'She's decided it's best if people know. You see, Carrie needs a bone marrow transplant to get well. Only, she hasn't found any new marrow that fits in with hers.' Jenny's face darkened. She felt a stab of fear, just thinking about Carrie.

Sarah sighed and gave a little shudder. 'I'm so sorry,'

she said. 'I know exactly how helpless and afraid you must feel.'

'Really?' Jenny said, surprised. How could Sarah know? she wondered.

'My younger sister.' Sarah was almost whispering. 'She had leukaemia, too.'

'Did she . . . get better?' Jenny asked.

'No, Jenny, she didn't,' Sarah said. 'She died. Nearly a year ago. I tried to help her. I donated bone marrow, but the match wasn't right.'

'Oh, that's awful,' said Jenny, wondering if the match of one person's marrow to another could ever be right. It didn't seem very likely.

'I'd like to meet Carrie – really I would,' Sarah said, changing the subject. She stood up. 'You will bring her in to the centre, when she wants to come?'

'Definitely. She'd like that,' Jenny said.

'I must get on with my work now,' Sarah smiled. 'It was nice to see you again, and to meet Fiona.'

'I'd better be getting back home, anyway,' Jenny said. 'I'll go and find the others.'

'OK, Jenny,' Sarah said. 'They're out through that door over there, at the pool. I really must stop chatting and get working. Thanks for coming in to see us.'

'We'll come again,' Jenny said.

'Oh, by the way – which hospital does Carrie go to, do you know?' Sarah asked.

'Yes, it's Greybridge Hospital,' Jenny said. 'Why?'

'No reason,' Sarah said, picking up a gannet and striding across to the sink. 'Bye for now.'

9

Over the next ten days, Jenny had more than enough to keep her busy. When she wasn't at school, or doing her homework, she divided her time between visiting Carrie and helping her father with the lambing.

In the middle of all the rushing around, Matt, Jenny's brother, came home for the weekend. She was helping Mrs Grace pack up a basket of food to take up to her father in the top field, when Matt's motor-bike roared into the courtyard. His smiling face appeared round the kitchen door.

'Matt!' cried Jenny. 'You made it! Where's Vicky?' Vicky was Matt's girlfriend. She was doing the same course as he was at Agricultural College. Matt slung his bag and helmet to the floor and ruffled Jenny's hair.

Jess was leaping around in excitement, getting under Matt's feet. 'Whoa! Steady boy!' he told the collie, rubbing his ears affectionately.

'Welcome home, Matt,' smiled Mrs Grace: 'Your dad *will* be pleased to see you!'

'Sorry I couldn't get back sooner,' Matt said, making a face. 'We all had to go on this field trip. There was no way of getting out of it.'

'Where's Vicky?' Jenny asked again.

'She's gone home to visit her mum and dad,' Matt told her, helping himself to a slice of cold meat from the chopping board. 'How's the lambing going?'

'No problems, so far. There are eight lambs in the lambing barn, all doing well,' Jenny reported. She realised she sounded a little flat. She gave her brother a bright smile.

'You look terrible, Jen.' Matt was frowning at her. 'Dad been working you hard, instead of me?' he joked. His blue eyes twinkled at her.

'Oh,' said Jenny vaguely, 'it's not that. It's just we've been having a . . . bit of a sad and difficult time lately.'

She reached for Jess, who was never far away. From under the table, he put his nose into her lap.

'What's this?' asked Matt, coming round and sitting beside Jenny. He peered into her face. 'Hey, what's up, little sis?' He looked concerned.

'I'll just take this lot out to the field, Jenny love,' Mrs Grace said, quietly. She lifted her basket. 'You have a chat with your brother. It *is* nice to have you home, Matt,' she added, and closed the door behind her.

'Carrie's got leukaemia.' Jenny said slowly.

'Oh . . . no,' Matt said. He looked stunned and was silent for a several seconds. 'That's nasty. Really nasty. Poor kid. Is she responding to treatment?'

'You mean the drugs?' Jenny asked. Matt nodded.

'I think so. She spent her second day in hospital this week. I've been visiting her at home each day. She feels sick most of the time so she can't go to school.'

'There's a good chance then – is there – that she'll get well again?' Matt said hopefully.

Jenny shrugged. 'Don't know, really,' she said. 'You see, Carrie had leukaemia before she came to live here. The drugs made her better that time. But now the sickness has come back.'

'Oh, poor girl,' Matt said.

117

'She needs a bone marrow transplant, Matt. Her own bone marrow is so damaged it can't mend itself. I want us all to be tested – you, Dad, Mrs Grace, even Vicky – all of us – to see if our marrow matches Carrie's,' Jenny was passionate. 'Will you do it?'

Matt blinked at her. She was squeezing his arm. 'Me?' he said. 'Us? But isn't Carrie more likely to find a match for her marrow among members of her own family?'

Jenny shook her head. 'She's tried all of them,' she said.

'Well, um, what does Dad say about this?' Matt wondered.

'I haven't asked him yet,' Jenny said. 'But I told Mrs Turner – and she's very grateful for the offer. At the moment, the doctors are looking through the register of donors – those are people who give their blood and marrow into a bank – to see if they can find anyone to match Carrie's.'

Matt gave a long, low whistle and sat back in his chair. 'Well, let's see what this donor bank turns up, shall we? If nothing comes of it, then, I'll get tested.'

'Thanks, Matt,' Jenny hugged him. 'I knew you would.'

'Right,' said Matt, standing up. 'I'm going to have a wash and get changed and then I'll go and give

Dad a hand with the ewes, OK?'

'OK.' She grinned.

Thoughts were racing around in Jenny's head. She took a moment to groom Jess's coat. His long fur had become tangled in places and he had a clump of burrs in his tail. Jess looked up as Jenny showed him the brush, then, obediently stretched out on his side on the kitchen floor. He gave a patient sigh.

'Yes,' Jenny chuckled. 'I know you're not particularly fond of being in the beauty parlour, but you're a mess!' She began to comb out his long hair and Jess rolled onto his back, allowing her to brush his tummy.

'Good boy,' she said, kissing the top of his nose. Next she tackled his knotty tail as he lay upside down. Jess sneezed, then cocked his ears. Suddenly, he rolled over and jumped up, giving a series of excited little yaps.

'What is it?' Jenny asked, as Jess shook himself all over. 'Don't think you're going to fool me into letting you off being groomed because . . .'

'Hi!'

Jenny looked round. Carrie was at the door.

'Carrie!' Jenny threw the brush aside. It went clattering across the floor. She leaped up and hugged her friend. Carrie was smiling, though her skin was ashen. She wore a French beret, set at a jaunty angle. Her hair had been cut short.

Jenny tried not to show her surprise. 'I like your hair.' she grinned at Carrie. 'It looks great.'

'Suits me, doesn't it?' Carrie spun around, her arms outstretched, pretending to be a fashion model.

'Why have you come? It's great to see you! How are you feeling?' The questions tumbled out. It was so good to see Carrie when she wasn't lying down looking bored.

'I'm feeling a bit better,' Carrie said. 'So I've come to see the lambs. Mum dropped me off.'

'We've got eight, or nine . . . I've lost count,' Jenny told her. 'Come on, let's go and see.'

Jess streaked ahead of Jenny, his tail waving happily as he bounded across the yard. Nell and Jake, Jess's parents, were dozing against the big barn in the morning sun. Nell looked up, and thumped her tail in the dirt in greeting. Jess nuzzled his mother under her ears, then looked around for Jenny.

'In here,' Jenny said, holding the door open for Carrie.

It was warm inside the barn. The only light came from the weak spring sunshine, slanting in through the cracks in the timber roof and criss-crossing on the straw on the floor. It smelled of freshly cut grass and lanolin, a combination Jenny loved. Fraser Miles had used the big bales of hay to make partitions for the pregnant ewes, providing a cosy and safe environment for the lambs to be born in.

'Why aren't they having their lambs out in the field?' Carrie asked, as the ewes turned their curious yellowy eyes on her.

'Sometimes Dad brings the first-time mothers in here,' Jenny replied. 'It's easier to keep an eye on them at night. Look!'

A lamb had been born moments before Jenny and Carrie had come into the barn. The ewe, her sides still heaving with her effort, had turned to investigate the tiny bundle that had slipped from her and was now lying still in the straw. She began to lick gently at it, rolling it over with her nose and lifting its tiny tail to inspect it all over.

'Oh that's amazing,' breathed Carrie, her hands clasped to her chest. 'Look how tiny it is! How sweet.'

'She's establishing a bond with her baby,' Jenny told her. 'If he ever gets separated from his mother out in the field, she will be able to find him.'

'Another successful birth,' said Fraser Miles, stepping up quietly from the shadows of the back of the barn. 'Hello, Carrie lass,' he added, warmly. 'How are you?'

'I'm OK, thanks, Mr Miles,' Carrie said. Fraser Miles stepped over into one of the hay bale partitions. Gently, he lifted a tiny dozing lamb – born, Jenny guessed, the day before. The little black head was still floppy and weak. He held it out to Carrie.

'Ah, it's so sweet,' she said, taking it into her arms. She stroked its curly coat. The lamb bleated pitifully, calling to its mother. Its tongue was pink against the coal-black of its face. 'You're gorgeous,' Carrie told the lamb. She sat down in the straw with it and put her finger gently into its mouth. The lamb began to suckle, making Carrie giggle.

'Any news, love?' Mr Miles asked gently. Jess had sidled up quietly. He lay down between Jenny and Carrie, his ears flat, head erect, his nose quivering, watching the tiny lamb with the dedication of a well-trained sheepdog. Jenny felt proud of Jess's strong instinct.

'Not really,' Carrie said, keeping her eyes on the lamb in her lap. 'I'm going to have a bone marrow transplant, if they can find someone whose marrow matches mine,' Carrie told him. 'They're still looking for a donor.'

'Right, lass,' smiled Fraser Miles. 'You'll keep us posted, won't you? On how it all goes – and if you need anything, any help . . .' he trailed off, looking uncertain. Then he brightened. 'Jenny, why don't you take advantage of the fact that Carrie is feeling better and take her to see those birds you rescued from Puffin Island?'

'Good idea!' cried Jenny. 'Can you come, Carrie?'

'Not today,' Carrie said. 'But I could go tomorrow. Are they open on Sunday?'

'Yes,' Jenny said, eagerly. 'Seven days a week.'

'I'll ask my mum, but I'm sure it'll be fine,' Carrie said. She bent over the tiny lamb. Its wobbly head was nodding sleepily. She smoothed its curly brow and smiled.

Jenny felt hopeful, looking at her friend. There was now a faint spread of colour in her cheeks. Perhaps there was a chance that she would soon be completely well again. In the meantime, there was tomorrow at the SSPCA centre, and introducing Sarah Taylor to Carrie, to look forward to.

10

Jenny woke up on Sunday feeling happier than she had for a long time. She was going to spend time with her best friend, away from Carrie's bedroom. She felt sure it would cheer Carrie up and take her mind off her illness for a while.

It was a brilliant day. The sky was clear and blue. Looking out of the window of her bedroom, she saw Matt herding the ewes out of the barn, getting them ready for the field. The lambs skittered about on their spindly legs, trying to keep up with their mothers, making a dreadful racket.

Nell and Jake were crouched in position, circling, ever-watchful, waiting to spring forward and ease the lambs back into line should they break free from the group. Jenny never tired of watching the dogs work. How she would love to reward their loyalty by bringing them into the house on a cold night and cuddling them up on a blanket beside the Aga stove. But rules were rules, she knew that. Nell and Jake were working dogs, not pets.

She thought of Jess, who'd be wanting his breakfast. Jenny dressed quickly, and hurried downstairs.

'He couldn't wait,' announced Ellen Grace, smiling. 'It was the smell of the bacon frying that did it.' Jenny burst out laughing. Jess had his nose in an enormous bowl. Without looking up, he wagged his tail hard. Then, having licked the last traces of egg and bacon from the dish, he rushed over to Jenny and licked her bare knee.

'Ooh! An eggy good morning kiss! Thanks, Jess,' she said with a giggle.

'Your father said to tell you that twins were born in the night,' Mrs Grace said.

'Oh, how lovely,' Jenny grinned. 'But I haven't time to see them this morning.'

'No, Carrie should be here soon,' Mrs Grace

remembered, glancing at her watch. 'How nice for you both to be out and about – just like the old days.'

'I'm so pleased she seems to be better,' Jenny said, putting a rasher of bacon between two slices of bread.

'Jenny,' Mrs Grace's tone was cautious. 'Remember that Carrie might have days when she's not feeling so good, won't you? It won't always be like this.'

'How do you mean?' Jenny frowned.

'Well, she'll have to have further treatment at the hospital. The drugs they give her will make her sick again,' Mrs Grace was gentle.

'I know,' Jenny sighed. She came over and gave Mrs Grace a hug. 'I won't get my hopes up too high, I promise. Or, at least, I'll try not to.'

Just then, Mrs Turner's flower-painted mini pulled into the drive, driven by Mr Turner.

'Here she is,' said Ellen Grace, as Jenny pulled away and dashed outside.

'Hello, Carrie,' she called. Her friend was wearing her woollen beret again. She was smiling, Jenny saw with relief, but she stayed in the car. 'Hello, Mr Turner.'

'Hello, Jenny,' he said, getting out. 'Do you fancy being driven down to the SSPCA centre? I'd like to get a look at these birds you rescued for myself.'

'Yes,' Jenny said. 'But, can Jess come? I hate to leave him and they don't really mind him being there.'

'Sure,' said Carrie's father. 'You jump into the back with him.' Jess looked at Jenny expectantly. He put his head to one side.

'In you get,' she instructed. Mr Turner pulled his seat forward and Jess slithered into the back.

Jenny got in beside him. 'Bye, Mrs Grace,' she called. Ellen's face appeared at the kitchen window. She blew Jenny a kiss and waved to Carrie.

'Have a good time,' she called.

'This is Carrie Turner,' Jenny told Sarah. Carrie grinned at the young woman and stuck out her hand.

'Nice to meet you,' she said.

Sarah shook hands. 'Hi, Carrie,' she said. 'I'm a bit filthy,' she added, looking down at her soiled, wet clothing. 'We've had a couple of very angry birds in the shower this morning!'

'You're doing a great job,' Mr Turner said. 'May I look around?'

'Sure,' Sarah said. 'We've had a good recovery rate since the oil spill. You'll find the more active birds out in the pool, over that way.' Sarah pointed.

'Thanks,' said Mr Turner, wandering away.

'How are you feeling?' Sarah had turned to Carrie.

'Jenny tells me that you have leukaemia.'

Jenny's heart turned over. Wasn't this just a bit too direct? Would Carrie be cross that Sarah knew? But, to her relief, Carrie smiled. 'Yes, that's right,' she said. 'But we're going to fight it, aren't we, Jen?'

'That's the spirit!' grinned Sarah. 'Now, are you two up for a bit of hard work?'

'Yes!' Jenny and Carrie spoke together. Carrie's eyes were bright.

'A few of the volunteers are taking some of the birds back to Puffin Island today. There are only traces of the oil left now, so it's quite safe. And I'm happy to report that they're well enough to go back to sea!' Sarah told them. 'Do you want to go along?'

'Oh, please!' Jenny begged. 'We'd love to . . . wouldn't we, Carrie?'

'Love to what?' said Mr Turner, coming over.

'Dad,' Carrie began, 'Sarah says some of the birds we saved from Puffin Island are ready to go back home today. Can we go along and see them set free? Please?'

'Yes, well, I expect so, if we take it gently, Carrie,' he said, quietly. 'We can go in our own boat, and follow the SSPCA boat out there, OK?'

'Oh, great,' Sarah was pleased. 'You've got your own boat!'

'Can Jess come too, Mr Turner?' Jenny asked. He grinned and nodded in reply. Jess was waiting in the reception room.

'Are you coming?' Carrie asked Sarah. Jenny could see Carrie had warmed immediately to Sarah.

'Um, no,' Sarah said. A shadow crossed her face. She glanced away. 'I've got an appointment, which I can't miss,' she said. 'But you go along, and you can tell me all about it when I next see you.'

'Oh . . .' Jenny was disappointed.

'I'll take you to where the birds are being loaded into our boat. You can meet Jack and Karen, our helpers. Then, just follow them out to Puffin Island.'

'Thanks,' Mr Turner said.

'I should say thank you to you!' Sarah laughed, linking arms with Carrie and Jenny. 'You did a great job bringing those birds to us the way you did. You've saved their lives. You deserve to see them go back to their island. Now, come with me.'

'I'll just go and get Jess,' Jenny said, and darted away to the reception area. Jess was lying down, his nose on his paws. He rushed towards Jenny when he saw her, and, as usual, greeted her as though he hadn't seen her in months.

'You're a good boy,' she told him. 'We're going out on the boat, Jess! Come on! Let's catch up with the others.' Jess barked, then trotted along at Jenny's side.

Outside, a trailer was being loaded with a cargo of boxed birds. It was hooked up to a van, marked with the logo SSPCA. Jenny spotted the two helpers, dressed in waterproof clothing and rubber-soled shoes. Carrie and Mr Turner were watching the operation with interest.

'This is Jenny Miles,' Sarah introduced her,' And Jess . . . this is Jack Castle and Karen Keane.'

'Hello,' Jenny said shyly. She and Carrie watched for a bit, then, Mr Turner suggested they set off to the quay at Cliffbay.

'We'll meet you there,' Jack said pleasantly.

'Have a good day!' Sarah said. 'I hope to see you again, soon.' She smiled at Carrie, who smiled back warmly.

Mr Turner drove them down to where his boat lay bobbing on a gentle swell of calm sea.

'Lovely day for a trip out to the island,' he said. 'Feeling all right, Carrie?'

'Yep,' Carrie said gamely. She adjusted her beret, and climbed into the boat. 'I'm glad it's calm, though,' she said. 'What a lovely, friendly person Sarah is,' she added.

'A charming girl,' Mr Turner agreed. He started

the engine and the boat began to shudder and shake.

'There they are!' Jenny said, pointing. 'There's Jack and Karen, and the SSPCA boat.' Jess looked too, to where Jenny was pointing. He lifted his nose to the wind, then jumped up onto the wooden seat that ran around the insides of the boat and settled comfortably.

'You're a real old sea dog at heart,' Jenny told him, ruffling his ears.

Mr Turner waved to Jack, then the boat began to lift and fall as it swung out towards the open sea. The early morning mist and the bright sunlight made it difficult to see the outline of Puffin Island, but Mr Turner knew exactly which direction to go.

'Those birds are going to get a happy surprise,' Carrie said. 'I'll bet they thought they would never see their little island ever again.' Jenny sat close to Carrie, watching her protectively. She didn't want Carrie to get too tired, or start to feel seasick.

'It's going to be great to watch them when they suddenly realise they are home, and free,' Jenny thought out loud.

Carrie nodded but didn't reply. She was quiet while the boat ploughed along through the water. From time to time, her eyelids started to close, then she opened them quickly and gave a little shake. Jenny said nothing, but her heart ached for her friend. How wonderful it would be if the doctors could find someone whose marrow matched Carrie's. Looking at her, Jenny wondered how much longer Carrie could wait.

'Nearly there,' she said, as Puffin Island came into view. Jess had been lying down. Now, he sat up and his tail began to swish happily from side to side.

When the boat had been safely anchored, Mr Turner disembarked, then he lifted Carrie down onto the shore, holding her in his arms like a baby. Jenny and Jess jumped onto the beach. Jenny's instinct was to dash across with Jess to where the SSPCA boat was unloading the boxes of birds, but she stopped herself. Carrie couldn't dash anywhere. When Mr Turner had put his daughter down, Jenny walked slowly, beside her. Jess seemed to sense this and he, too, walked sedately next to Jenny.

'Most of the oil has gone,' she said, looking around her. 'Isn't that great?'

'I can still see a few little patches of it,' Carrie said.

'You know, Puffin Island was very lucky to have escaped the major spill further along the coast,' Mr Turner said. 'The result of a spill near this bird sanctuary could have been a disaster.'

Jack and Karen had reached Puffin Island before

them. They had already lined up the boxes along the shoreline. As Jenny drew closer, she could see the cardboard was shifting about eerily on the shingle as the healthy birds inside struggled for their freedom. There was the sound of pecking, and the occasional squawk and call.

'Ready?' said Karen, to Jack.

'I certainly am,' he grinned. They began to open the flaps of the boxes.

Within seconds, the alert and frantic heads of a variety of birds – scoters and guillemots, puffins and razorbills – were popping up comically from their boxes. Beaks opened, heads swivelled, bright eyes blinked, wings flapped – and the boxes toppled over as the birds began to break free. Half running, half flying, they made for the sea, cawing and calling in panic.

Jenny was thrilled by it. She looked around for Jess and noticed that he had crouched low, and was inching forward, circling, his head moving from side to side, trying to keep an eye on the scrabbling, fleeing birds.

'Oh, Jess!' Jenny collapsed with laughter. 'Don't worry about it! These aren't sheep, they're birds.'

'That's his instinct coming out,' observed Mr Turner. 'You can't keep a good sheepdog down!'

'You're a sweetie,' said Carrie, patting his head.

Some of the birds had spread their wings and taken to the sky. They wheeled around, their beaks opening and closing, as though celebrating their freedom. Others were bobbing about in the waves, ducking their heads gleefully into the water.

'What a marvellous sight,' said Mr Turner.

'They're so happy to be back!' Jenny said. She was thinking how Carrie might have reacted to this scene before she'd become ill. The old Carrie would have whooped and shouted with joy; she would have done cartwheels across the sand. This Carrie stood watching quietly, her thin arms folded across her

tummy, a fixed, sad smile on her face.

'Come on, love,' said Mr Turner, putting a gentle hand on her shoulder. 'We'll get you home, now. Let's say our goodbyes, and get back in the boat.'

Carrie nodded. 'I'm so glad we came,' was all she said.

Back in Cliffbay harbour, Jenny helped Mr Turner to lock up the boat and pull the awnings down over the deck. Carrie sat down on a patch of grass, her arm round Jess's back. Her hand moved gently across his coat but her expression was blank and sad. Jess sat looking at her, as if he, too, was perplexed at the change in her.

'I'll bring some schoolwork round to your house this afternoon, if you like,' Jenny said brightly.

Carrie smiled and nodded and they got into the car. She was silent all the way home. Jenny didn't know what to say, so she said nothing. There was little point in forcing a merry conversation just for the sake of it.

As Mr Turner came slowly through the gates of Windy Hill, Jess barked happily.

'Looks like you've got a visitor,' observed Carrie's father.

Jenny peered out of the window of the mini as

they came to a stop in the yard. A car she hadn't seen before was parked there.

Carrie's head was resting against the back of the seat, and she sat up. 'Who?' she asked, without much interest.

'I don't know . . .' Jenny began, as the kitchen door opened.

Ellen Grace came out onto the top step. Jenny could see right away that she had been crying. Her heart squeezed tight in her chest. Standing behind her was Mrs Turner. Matt and Mr Miles were standing at the kitchen window. Jenny was relieved to see that her brother was smiling broadly. But, what on earth had happened? Why was Carrie's mum here? Why was everyone looking out for them?

'Let's get you out,' said Mr Turner, helping Carrie from the back of the car. 'It looks like your mother's here to meet us. Fraser must be having a little party . . .' Jess slipped past Carrie and up the steps.

'Mrs Grace, Mrs Turner . . .' Jenny ran forward. 'Is anything the matter?' Mrs Turner ran past Jenny and over to the car. She put her arms around her daughter and gave her a long, tight hug.

'We've had some news,' she told Carrie, her eyes filling with tears. 'Some wonderful news. Come inside, all of you.'

Jenny stood in the doorway of the kitchen and gaped. There was Sarah Taylor sitting at the pine table as though she was a regular visitor at Windy Hill. She was smiling gently, fussing Jess, who had gone over to greet her.

'Hello, Sarah!' Jenny said, surprised. 'Well, gosh . . . how . . . what . . .?'

'Perhaps,' Mr Miles said, 'we ought to let Sarah explain.'

'Good idea,' Matt piped up.

'I'll make some more tea,' said Mrs Grace.

Sarah went over to Carrie who was holding her mother's hand tightly, frowning in confusion.

'I've had some news today – from my doctor,' Sarah started. 'And I couldn't wait to share it. So I found out where the Turners live and then Carrie's mum and I came over here to find you all.' She took a long, shuddering breath.

Carrie stared at her, bewildered. Jenny had started to think that they had won an award for rescuing the birds.

'You see . . .' Sarah paused. 'My bone marrow is the exact match for yours, Carrie . . .And I'm going to be your donor.'

'What?' shouted Jenny, making Jess's ears prick up. He hurried over to her side and put up his paw.

Carrie sat down suddenly on the nearest chair, blinking.

'I was tested a year ago,' Sarah explained. 'It was when my sister was ill with leukaemia. I wanted to donate some marrow then, but I wasn't the right match for her. I was bitterly disappointed and, after Katie died, I felt as though I had failed her. Anyway, for a while, I couldn't face having any reminders of what had happened and so I withdrew my name from the National Register – that's the bank where they keep all donors on file. Then I heard about you, Carrie. And, as the test was already done, and you and I have the same doctor, all that had to be done was to check to see if my marrow was compatible with yours.'

'And it is?' Carrie said slowly, obviously struggling to take in what Sarah was saying. 'It really is?'

'It's a perfect match!' Mrs Turner cried, throwing her arms round Mr Turner's waist.

He put his cheek on the top of her head and squeezed his eyes shut. 'How can we begin to thank you, Sarah?' he said. His voice came out as a croak.

'I'm so pleased to be able to help.' Sarah smiled. 'I felt so . . . hopeless, when my sister . . .' She broke off, as Carrie reached up and gave her a hug.

'Thank you!' Carrie whispered. Then, looking

round, Carrie caught Jenny's eye. She rushed over and grabbed Jenny round the waist. 'I'm going to get well! I'm going to get better!' she chanted, dancing Jenny around the kitchen. Jess barked gleefully, his tail going in circles.

'Mind that teapot!' warned Mrs Grace, loudly, wending her way through the noisy crowd with her tray. Jenny looked at Carrie. Two bright spots of pink had appeared in her cheeks, bringing her face alive, and her eyes flashed with a sparkle Jenny hadn't seen in days. She didn't know whether to laugh or cry with relief and happiness.

Mrs Grace had found room for the tray on the table. Jenny saw her take a tissue out of her sleeve and dab at her eyes. She went over and gave her a hug.

'A happy day!' sniffed Ellen Grace. 'What a *happy* day, Jen, love.'

'It is,' Jenny said, kissing Mrs Grace on a cheek wet with tears of joy. 'One of the very best.'